LOST LOVES

LOST LOVES

A Novel

Andrew Grof

Sunstone books may be purchased for educational, business, or sales promotional use.
For information please write: Special Markets Department, Sunstone Press,
P.O. Box 2321, Santa Fe, New Mexico 87504-2321.
Book and cover design › Vicki Ahl
Body typeface › Goudy
Printed on acid-free paper
∞
eBook 978-1-61139-434-4

Library of Congress Cataloging-in-Publication Data

Grof, Andrew, 1946-
Lost loves : a novel / by Andrew Grof.
   pages ; cm
ISBN 978-1-63293-087-3 (softcover : alk. paper)
I. Title.
PS3607.R6343L67 2015
813'.6--dc23

2015032259

Sunstone Press is committed to minimizing our environmental impact on the planet. The paper used in this book is from
responsibly managed forests. Our printer has received Chain of Custody (CoC) certification from: The Forest Stewardship Council™
(FSC®), Programme for the Endorsement of Forest Certification™ (PEFC™), and The Sustainable Forestry Initiative® (SFI®).

The FSC® Council is a non-profit organization, promoting the environmentally appropriate, socially beneficial and economically
viable management of the world's forests. FSC® certification is recognized internationally as a rigorous environmental and social
standard for responsible forest management.

WWW.SUNSTONEPRESS.COM
SUNSTONE PRESS / POST OFFICE BOX 2321 / SANTA FE, NM 87504-2321 /USA
(505) 988-4418 / ORDERS ONLY (800) 243-5644 / FAX (505) 988-1025

For Caryl
and
For Arthur

"I can't recall a time in my life
when I was not in love with someone."

Here we go. How many?

That's exactly right.

How many words left, because words like memories, at times we seem to pull them out of nowhere, or they us, it hardly matters, the main thing is there are only a finite number, no, I can't emphasize this enough, A FINITE NUMBER, which applies to everything in sight and sound and smell and touch and taste, I just hope you're following this, that we're more or less on the same page, theories of endless returns, of infinite beginnings and endings, forever expanding or disappearing and reappearing universes have never touched me where I lived, nothing I could sink my teeth into, for me the here and now all that ever mattered, notions of infinity left me colder than a dead mackerel, you see, you see right now I'm talking about nothing less than time itself, the very finiteness of things and one's way of running out, no, I don't think you could argue the opposite, and one's last, one's final efforts to grasp, to hold on, the thing is we arrive baggageless into this world and then in time and with time the baggage accumulates to take on an immense and even terrifying importance, we mean to lose nothing of what we've accumulated, mentally and every other way, our naked existence no longer sufficient, our dreams and hopes no longer enough to carry us from one day or night to the next, scaling down, becoming ghosts of ourselves not an option, we become fearful of letting our memories of gains, losses, loves fade into limbo, still, what other choice in the end, we are facing a blank wall through which we'll find it impossible to pass, and, yes, we can even envision a time when no one will recall our single, individual, solitary passage through life, the tremendous SO WHAT? of our existence, but I'm just saying, simply trying to clarify things to myself.

Bear with me.

Just for the time being.

That's all I'm asking.

Even if at times my musings may strike you as contradictory or even totally clueless.

I'm entitled to a hearing I think.

We all are.

The flowers, all the flowers are killing me.

Stinking up the room.

The magnolias, the forget-me-nots and the roses, of course, the roses the worst, no stems without thorns, a rose by any other name and all the rest, no, I would prefer them without names, no names at all, in fact I want them out of here, stems, blooms, thorns and all, I don't care what's to become of them, tossed or given away, it simply doesn't matter to me.

I gesture to communicate, to make my feelings known. Useless of course.

All the doctors, nurses, my various visitors clueless as far as I can tell, what do their smiling faces have to do with my own, their steady hands with my own trembling ones, they're all in season while I'm already practically out of it might be another way of putting it, although now and again, I'm not denying, with certain people there does appear to be a glimmer of understanding, here we are, here we go, yes, something along those lines, but they arrive and leave while I simply stay put, I can't emphasize this too strongly, I SIMPLY STAY PUT, my animate or inanimate sounds occasionally accompanied by spittles and drools, "There, there, let me wipe it off," but, really, it doesn't matter, "God bless and keep you, Viktor," sometimes, often, practically always it's annoying as hell.

The sun at an angle.

'God bless and keep the sun,' they may as well say.

Or any and all angles, right, acute, obtuse, the more angles the better as far as I'm concerned, and the more blessings the merrier, they do neither harm nor good as far as I can tell, I gesture with my hand to indicate the lines of light that crisscross, dissect and separate my room into unequal sections, "Yes, yes, we see," they don't of course, their acquaintance with light and lines and angles superficial at best, given my interminable hours of observation, of concentration I'm the only expert around here, a regular Pythagoras compared to any one of them, but none of this matters, it really doesn't, I'm simply stating the obvious.

Something else about the sun.

I hope you don't mind my going on.

The source of all life of course, so one either has to love or hate it, and, no, contrary to what you might expect I for one have always loved it, no, don't let my current state of indifference detract from my intense, even immense emotions, passions of the past, to say that I once worshipped and adored the sun as well as life's myriad manifestations is no mere exaggeration, in other words my present appearance no indication of the force with which I once embraced life, the sun just a single and singular example, that I was once a passionate man you could hardly deduce from my current mental and physical state, as a matter of fact, "Think, Viktor, please, think," friends would often advise, but everything united in me let's just say, mind and body acting in unison to grab, to swallow, to fully digest, I denied myself nothing, embraced the world in both proper and improper fashions, gorged myself on life in other words, my appetites, my loves with no discernible bounds.

Satisfied?

I for one hardly ever was, feared satisfaction like the plague, moved from experience to experience, adventure to adventure like one both obsessed and possessed, the fallen angels of my being in glorious technicolor, like Satan himself, who, you might recall, was Lucifer once, the very light of the heavens before he took on God Himself and refused to worship the suffering Christ.

Enough, though. Yes. Enough I think.

The sun. Yes, let's return. I was thinking, talking about the sun.

The truth of the matter is that in my current state I am no more fond of the light than I am of the dark, each with its particular advantage and disadvantages, I often find it easier to think, to dream, to concentrate in the dark, although the difference between dreaming and waking negligible in my case, I may well be dreaming while fully awake or awake while dreaming, impossible at times to tell the difference, at any rate I'm a light sleeper with the sights and sounds of both the present and the past easily invading my so-called dreams.

I think you understand. I just hope you do.

Debilitated now.

Lying, sitting up, occasionally walking, but, no, mostly lying here I feel like a man condemned to a private cell, a cell both within and without, and condemned without justification, yes, important to note, unless life itself a justification for its own decay and eventual destruction, I have neither the desire nor the skill to pursue such a line of thought, 'Let it be,' I often say to myself in my darkest moments, or, simply, 'Let be,' like Hamlet near the end of his play that basically revolved around no one but himself.

"Let's go home," I said to a woman the other day, my wife, my last I was told although I had no clear recollection of her or of the home I meant to return to, I said it simply to bring a smile to her face which was anything but unpleasant, her full lips and dark eyes gentle across my sunken features.

I admit it. I would have loved to recall her then, yes, even a single moment of the two of us together would have sufficed, yes, I even tried to visualize her naked beneath her attractive dress, 'Undress,' I was even on the verge of telling her, 'let me see what you really look like,' but even a man in my condition aware of certain proprieties, boundaries which might be dangerous, even fatal to cross.

Her hair like dead leaves I thought then to mitigate her nearness, her upsetting physical presence.

Delicate hands and teeth like freshwater pearls.

"No, don't come any closer," I told her.

"I'm Samantha," she smiled. "Don't you know me?"

Names ephemeral, weightless as far as I was concerned. Have they always been? I only wished I'd known.

But.

Aside from my initial confusion and total lack of recollection the visit a pleasant one. We talked of Beethoven and Mahler, as a matter of fact she grew quite animated at the very mention of these names which made me think she might have had something to do with music or that I had in the past, in fact at one point I got a very clear picture of a bright room with a grand piano near the window, I saw myself sitting upright by the keys with Samantha leaning naked over me, an incongruous picture to be sure, but not everything in one's imagination has to correspond to so-called actual realities.

As the visit progressed we sat in silence for a spell, and it was in that very silence that I felt closest and farthest from her, now the one, now the other, as if silence or a simple absence of words had this power to both fuse and part us.

"Is there anything you need?" she asked, but by then it was a stranger's voice asking a strange, even ridiculous question, and, "No, I have everything I need," I replied without looking at her and meaning nothing, no, absolutely nothing at all, and she nodded as though she understood, and that very nod made her fade as if from view, it certainly seemed like that at the time.

And she left.

Shortly afterwards she left.

Now and again.

'How much time left?' I muse to myself.

Moments when time as if with nothing to do with me, time as the past, present and possible future, in other words now and again I feel myself in a certain state of inner timelessness which has nothing, no, absolutely nothing to do with the passage of time without, although this in no way negates the absurd inevitability of chronological time, in fact I'm as keenly aware of this as is humanly possible.

"Ah, you've had another accident, Mister Truman," the nurse tells me. "I wish you would have rung for me."

Viktor. She never calls me Viktor.

Ah, well, I can only suppose a certain formality, a distance an aid in the conduct of her work.

"Win some, lose some," I smile at her.

No.

I won't deny myself my little games, the occasional soiling of my bed fairly high on the list, after all if still alive then certain unavoidable manifestations of life no matter how disgusting, at any rate she manages to keep her disgust to herself, an efficient, a dedicated worker I must admit, and I harbor no strong objections to being handled like an inanimate object by her capable hands, 'Signs of things to come,' I say to myself and thoroughly enjoy the process.

But were we or were we not contemplating, discussing time?

I think we were.

And if time then, what? Why, death of course. Time with a definite beginning and end as far as I'm concerned, in fact I often amuse myself by picturing a river now broad, now narrow, now slow, now swift moving, it all depends, but the river is time, you see, and carrying everything and everyone as it flows, and then, yes, death, the end, which is nothing more than a stepping out of that river, quite simple when you think of it, no need for more complex analyses, for becoming maudlin, excessively emotional about the matter.

And something else occurs to me just now.

Our deaths our most personal and individual things about us, our truest and most solitary acts with no one to assist us or take our places, yes, fake the rest of our lives along with everyone else that fakery will do us no good when it's time to call it quits, yes, it's in death we truly become ourselves or what we were meant to be, and although I have no clear idea what that might be I fully intend to embrace my death even as it embraces me, but whether this is of some aid in bearing my current state I have no idea, sometimes yes but at others no, definitely not.

Enough.

"Here, let me help you with those."

I insist on wearing shirts with buttons, nothing worse, nothing more embarrassing than those hospital gowns open to the back, I refuse to be draped into one, and if this leads to a certain amount of fumbling, of complicating my life, so be it. I will not be dictated to in this matter, in others, yes, I have no choice, but, no, not in this.

Ah, those lovely zippers and buttons of the past.

Whose, you may well ask.

Does it matter?

But the memory of the very sounds of zippers unzipping and the feel of buttons unbuttoning bring certain images to mind, how can they not, treasures, yes, all those treasures of the flesh hidden then revealed, the warmth as well as the scents issuing forth, believe me, I rushed nothing in those days, all my so-called seductions carefully calculated and choreographed with each step as essential and enjoyable as the next, and, at the risk of appearing to be boasting, may I now suggest that no single lover of mine was ever left dissatisfied, yes, with me as a person, quite possibly, but as a lover or with the act of love itself, no, never, please, bear this in mind to mitigate any future harsh judgments, the times, places and circumstances hardly ever withstanding, indeed, I am reminded of Chaucer' s prioress, was it, with her golden AMOR VINCIT OMNIA necklace, yes, now and again, and in my case quite often love did conquer all, conquests of others but of myself as well, no, don't ask me to explain, suffice it to say that I never deceived, faked, simulated in any of my amorous encounters, as in death, supposedly, I became fully myself and desired nothing more than for my partners to do the same, I have not only my countless memories but my current hard-on to testify, a joyous participant in the dance of life as I then thought of it, and still do, no, my attitude toward this hasn't changed, not one iota, even now I don't think it offensive or even unseemly to occasionally expose myself to some of the nurses, it hardly matters that they find the spectacle of a hard penis attached to decrepit body ludicrous or pitiable at best, let them smile all they want, think what they will, I simply want them to see what they're missing, to pull them a bit into my past and myself along with them.

Ah, but how easily we surrender ourselves to our bodily desires, the very voluptuousness of life all around, even in my present state I look on this as a blessing, not a curse, affairs of the mind much more of a curse than those of the body I've always felt, the Greeks' legacy of the religion of the mind highly questionable, and this from someone who was always enamored of the Greeks, their sense of proportion, beauty, their enviable attitude toward their all-too-human gods.

Never mind.

Certain cries in the night.

Human, not animal, and so much harder to accept, to bear, the collective pains of this place bursting like buboes in the night, I make myself listen, hear without the least possibility of doing anything about them, juxtapose these to the cries of women in the throes of ecstasy, 'Yes, this too is life,' I tell myself, two sides of the same coin, at times I feel one needs to know no more than this to comprehend life, I let the sounds carry me to uncertain times and places in the past, they wash over me like waves which often make breathing difficult if not entirely impossible.

"Hold my hand."

Terrific.

Or.

"Lick my ears."

The same.

Or.

"Kiss me, kiss me down there."

Yes.

We all know what we want out of love if not necessarily life, we know it innately, instinctively or at any rate our bodies do, it only remains for our minds to be kept at bay, to be held back from interfering, a certain liberation of the flesh and the spirit with nothing, absolutely nothing to do with the mind, let me repeat, ABSOLUTELY NOTHING TO DO WITH THE MIND, we, all of us simply need someone to throw open the doors, the window, to loosen the bolts of self-restraint, yes, if I have done nothing else in my life I have certainly done that for any and all my amorous partners, I merely mention this in passing without any notion of pride or sense of accomplishment, it came to me as naturally as breathing, swallowing and blinking my eyes.

And what, yes, what remains of this now?

Certain images, words like the ones above, the images birthing the phrases or the other way around, difficult to tell, but a man in my condition, a beggar in fact certainly can't afford to be a chooser, and I'm grateful for any and all combinations of words and images that seem to arise as if out of nowhere with no conscious effort on my part.

Life's very last gifts perhaps. Rewards for my having struggled and survived as long as I have without calling it quits along the way.

Oh, on any number of occasions.

Not worth going into just now.

My eyes wide open.

Just now I mean.

At times I see with a great deal, an almost painful degree of clarity, during the day but often at night as well, the most ordinary objects assuming an extraordinary distinctness as to shape, color and tactility, the inanimate as if becoming animate then, and, yes, with the accompanying feeling that everything is precisely what it is and was meant to be, that everything fits with nothing, ABSOLUTELY NOTHING OUT OF PLACE, those moments brief of course, how could they be otherwise, I would not be able to carry on, to survive for long in those particular states of intense attention.

"Are you all right, Mister Probst?"

Rigid.

Yes, for those blinding moments of concentration I suppose I am, my nurse forever fearing the worst, of having me slip through her fingers without her possible interference.

Yes.

But appearances not withstanding, the fact is that during those blinding moments I am more alive than at any others, everywhere and nowhere, both here and not here if I may put it that way. I understand her concern of course. I would act no differently in her place.

"Are you all right, Mister Probst?"

"What?"

In the end I manage to wink at her and let her make of this what she will.

Ah, the tedious, the endless routines, instructions, directions.

Most unnatural to say the least.

"Time to turn over."

Or.

"Time to piss, to fart, to shit," or whatever.

'Point of order,' I want to interrupt her, or, 'Time out,' or, 'Just once down the corridor if you don't mind.'

No, it would be difficult to bear all this without some humor no matter how slight, a trickster god the only one I ever recognized and was even occasionally fond of.

The windows wide open.

"Smell the air, Ms. Boyer," I tell her. "The trees, the whole world in bloom."

Or something along those lines.

I always call her Ms. Boyer exactly the way she persists in calling me Mister Probst, I would readily change if she would and call her Anne or Anna, I'm not sure which, but I will not be the one to initiate, to cross the barrier she's so carefully erected.

"I have no time for such foolishness."

Yes.

It may well be that Ms. Boyer or Anne or Anna is my very last challenge and I hers, that we are here precisely for this purpose, I in my useless and miserable state and she in her useful but equally miserable one, to break through each other's defenses to arrive, where, no, I'm not sure, but somewhere else than we currently find ourselves.

"A slight temperature."

"How slight?"

'Inhale, exhale, inhale, exhale.'

Groucho of course with a horse as a patient.

Which I'm tempted, but only tempted to share with her.

But.

My sense of smell practically shot to hell, my lungs frequently on the verge of collapsing, I'm never quite sure, and so on and so forth.

My litany of ills which have everything but at times as if nothing to do with me, at any rate I have never been partial to litanies of any sort, they come at you from all corners, from everywhere at once and leave you no time to ponder, to reflect.

Indeed.

"Whose life is this anyway?" I once theatrically confronted Ms. Boyer after one of her more unbearable harangues, meaning whose dream or whose death, I'm not sure which, a blank, uncomprehending stare was her only response, I let it go, pursued the joke, the matter went no further at the time.

Her hair, her body, yes, even her way of carrying herself betraying a certain stiffness of spirit. The very set of her face.

No, I'm not judging, merely observing, one of the near total blessings of my life has been this remarkable absence of a judgmental attitude, which is not to say I haven't observed and drawn inescapable conclusions, I still do of course, in fact what else but observe in my present state, my current condition, one of my prime sources of entertainment if I dare call it such.

"Let your hair down, Ms. Boyer," I once said to her apropos nothing at all. Out of the clear blue like that which I felt more effective at the time.

No response.

Not even a look, a shake or nod of the head.

"Sway, Ms. Boyer. A bit of swaying in your walk might do both of us a world of good.'

The same. No response.

Yes.

The challenge of Ms. Boyer a most frustrating yet intriguing one, there are other nurses on the floor of course, younger and of a more pliant and agreeable disposition, but for some reason I don't care to analyze, too weak I suppose, I have set my eyes, my mind and heart on Ms. Boyer as though she were the last woman on earth and I the last man. Which we may well be. I'm just saying.

Once in a while, not often, but every now and again I try to picture her stark naked as she mindfully carries out her assigned tasks, so far all attempts have ended in dismal failure, the stiffness extends well beneath her smart, her spotless uniform, and even in my present state a stiff female nude more than I care to handle.

Unsettling to say the least.

I observe myself observing, watch myself even as I watch her, it helps pass the time, my so-called waking hours, 'If you succeed with her,' I occasionally tell myself, 'then you will have had your last, perhaps most important success of your life, some sort of final goal accomplished, some somewhere finally arrived at,' ah, but where, yes, that is the question, and it is highly questionable that then I will die a happy or at any rate contented man, the whole thing quite puzzling and beyond any satisfying solution.

Yes.

Curious.

Yes.

But curious how at times she appears to come at me from all corners, from every direction at once, it's all in my imagination of course but no less real for all that, her very presence now exhausting, now exhilarating me, once or twice I have attempted to carry her into my dreams, not as impossible as it sounds for a man of heightened sensitivities, yes, and there to have done with her once and for all, a physical as well as a spiritual encounter such as neither of us had ever experienced before, yes, and then there would be nothing of any concern left to my waking hours, just a blissful emptiness in which she could carry on with her assigned tasks and I with mine, she with her mindless activities and I with my mindful dying.

The body a most curious mechanism.

I have felt and perhaps even known this ever since I was a child, yes, precocious in some things but not the ones that truly counted, no matter, but aware of the mind body dilemma at a fairly young age let's just say, the mind appearing to be one thing and the body with its monotonous needs and functions something altogether different, not that unknowingly I was then or would ever become anything of a Cartesian with its mindless embrace of an impossible duality, no, all of it an entire, a single, a whole package if you will, but puzzling, annoying and quite beyond my ability to comprehend. A finite, an imperfect, a forever decaying body birthing a seemingly unbounded consciousness, a nearly limitless mind.
Allies or enemies, at times I feel it impossible to decide.

Yes. The body forever running down with the mind perpetually racing on.

Take my current, my present physical state.

Why not?

On the surface various scabs, growths, wounds that refuse to heal, certain obvious discolorations as if tracing and recording the very passage of time, and then the deeper we go, the more we descend, penetrate, the more complex the problems encountered, the various organs I'm talking about, kidneys, liver, lungs, intestines, and the heart, yes, of course the heart with its uneven although to me highly interesting rhythms, I dare say its peculiar and or precarious beatings entertaining me at times, ah, is the observer the observed or is there an unsurpassable distance between the two, a terrific question as far as I'm concerned, although it doesn't do

20

to pause and ponder too long, please, let me be perfectly clear about this, ONE MUST NEVER PONDER ANYTHING TOO LONG, if I would have had a motto in life this would have been it, over the years, the decades I've had too many friends, acquaintances who pondered themselves into states of lethargy or worse, a bottomless sarcasm that admits of no possible victories in life no matter how small, but here I am doing the very thing I'm ranting against, pondering much too much with no particular end in sight.

Yes.

The various tricks, subterfuges and deceptions of the mind, its pitiful mockery and half-hearted imitation of the trickster god no doubt, I for one trust the mind, my own and anyone else's no farther than I can throw it, of some unquestionable use for survival, I'm not arguing, but as for solving our deeper problems of existence let's just say, no, it's practically useless, I'll take the decaying, the decrepit body any time of the day or night.

Which reminds me.

Russell's nasty old grandmother's single sentence dismissal of philosophy. "What is mind, no matter; what is matter, never mind."

Good, right? Humorous but highly effective. Yes.

So, where were we?

Time passes let's just say and be done with it.

All of us its unquestioned captives, no single one of us ever escapes except for our final exits, in fact we are made of time stuff, our fears, hopes, desires and our passions, our very thoughts in fact, all the doubts that continually assail us, all our peculiar certainties to which we so pathetically cling.

"Do you think we're made of time stuff?" I asked Ms. Boyer, my unflappable nurse the other day.

She pretended not to hear.

Such questions well beyond her abilities to handle, to comprehend.

Yes.

Time passes let's just say and let it go at that.

The tick-tock sounds of my night table clock annoy me, the gift of someone with a wicked sense of humor, it would be easy enough to get rid of, to give or simply toss it away, but why should I toss anything away, even something as annoying as a ticking clock, I who in my present woeful state am firmly dedicated to the resurrection and preservation of everything of my past, a most frustrating and useless endeavor of course, but, no, let me hang on to everything of my past as well as my present for as long as I can, my final letting go promises to be a definitive one, no doubt I will be as empty-handed then as the day I was born.

A woman.

Someone from the past called on the phone.

A hateful mechanism, I rarely pick up, this sort of effortless invasion worse than an insult, an annoying reflection in a distorting mirror in which one can hardly hope to glimpse one's true reflection.

"Are you up for visitors?"

I recognized neither the voice nor the name, although, I must admit, something of the warmth of a shared past did manage to come across.

"Mornings are best," I told her, "the early mornings best."

I don't know why I said that, for my lucidity, my powers of concentration vary from day to night, from hour to hour in fact, it is something over which I seem to exercise little or no power, still, it made me feel good to have lied to her in this innocuous fashion, to have specified a time of day for her so-called visit, no doubt it gave me some semblance of control which for the most part I rarely possess.

In the interval between the present and her impending visit I let her name, Kaethe, play loosely in my mind, clinging to and embracing its very sound, its syllables as it were, no, it was of no help, ABSOLUTELY NO HELP AT ALL, Kaethe like a stranger, some sort of representative of a past that now belonged only to her and no longer to me, her visit suspect to my eyes, she would come as if to connect or reconnect with herself and not at all with me.

For days I felt powerless in my bed, like one of those inanimate targets in a shooting gallery. Hit or miss she would take her shots and depart, the target, the shooting gallery existed solely for her benefit and not at all for mine.

A pleasant, although not entirely unexpected surprise.

While catholic, my taste in women has always bordered on the elegant, the elusive.

After the initial greeting followed by a more than perfunctory embrace, I took my time studying her. An invalid's prerogative if ever there was one.

Long of face and hair and limbs, she reminded me of those late eighteenth century aristocratic British women who in their portraits appeared to be both fully present as well as well beyond the reach of their viewers.

"Don't tell me you don't recall," she said at one point. I didn't.

In fact throughout her visit I said very little and let her do much if not most of the talking, after all it was she who came to unveil and repossess her past and mine and not the other way around, although I must admit I was more than willing to be taken along any ride she chose as I was no doubt in the past as well.

"Look at me, Viktor. Please, please, open your eyes and look at me.

From time to time I did my best of course. Made her appear and disappear as if at will. And.

I must admit that now and again I felt certain waves of emotion wash over me, emotions accompanied or even caused by certain images from the past, images of a bright and airy apartment with windows stretching from floor to ceiling, a bed as soft and wide as the sea on a calm afternoon, Kaethe's warm body like some sunlit and welcoming playground in which I, we played hide and seek and other similar games, jealous, yes, I must confess I became jealous of these images and had no desire to share them with her, she, no doubt, harbored her own images which only vaguely resembled mine, yes, I was quite sure, at any rate how could the Kaethe of the present, of that morning compete with my very own Kaethe of the past, indeed, here was a near-total stranger masquerading as one of the great loves of my life, and although time had been kind to her, much kinder than to me for example, it became frustrating and even painful to compare this Kaethe with the one from the past, in other words my interest in the present Kaethe only of a mild and passing sort, I listened to her stories of course, how could I not, replete with any number of gestures and exclamations, "Would you believe, Viktor," she kept repeating, "would you believe?" the stories of her varied interests and apparently satisfying life left me cold and with an increasingly assertive headache, add to this a certain shortness of breath which I only partially simulated, in the end I had no choice but to ring for the nurse, for Ms. Boyer to rescue me from this unhealthy collision of the past with the present, a single glance at my posture and features sufficient for her to realize the extent of my suffering, "I'm afraid I must ask you to leave now," she definitively pronounced, and, no, never was I more grateful to her than at that particular moment, yes, there is no arguing with authority, Kaethe's tales of her adventurous life effectively cut short, "Ah, but we're just getting reacquainted, just catching up," she complained, to which, "I'm afraid it'll have to be postponed," Ms. Boyer simply remarked, I could have hugged her then, pulled her down on my sweat-soaked bed, Kaethe bent down and kissed me full on my parched, my cracked lips, credit where credit's due, but not before she turned around to give a little wave that usually only children are capable of making, I managed a nod and a smile before shutting my eyes and carrying the exhausting efforts of that nod and smile into my personal darkness without boundaries.

Is one ever truly ready for life?
Or for death for that matter?
I for one have never been, I'm speaking of the past as well as the present, any number of practice runs as though at some stage of my living and dying practice was bound to make perfect, it never did of course, mere attempts at living and dying never quite the same as actually living and or dying, and, yes, the two somehow intricately related I suspect and have all along, accomplish the one with no reservations, hesitations and you will no doubt satisfactorily accomplish the other, I for one never have, doubts, hesitations, second thoughts about nearly every activity of mine in the past, never the actor without the observer in other words, with the two as if separate and mutually exclusive entities, the actor never fully the actor and the observer never entirely the observer, yes, perhaps the heights of sexual passion the single and singular exceptions, but what are those fleeting moments compared to the rest of all the other seemingly endless ones, but, don't take these musings more seriously than they deserve, they may well be the products of a feverish imagination, a hundred and three at the last measuring, although numbers indicative of nothing as far as I'm concerned, certain states of the body and soul quite beyond quantification or measurement of any sort.

Still.

Just now my left arm stiff, practically useless, more or less the same for my left leg, "Nothing to worry about," Ms. Boyer assures me, "such things quite normal for someone in your condition," yes, but precisely what condition is that, I have been given too many diagnoses for any one of them to be the right, the absolutely correct one, do you understand, THE ABSOLUTELY CORRECT ONE, "Such things come and go," she adds as if as an aside to herself, her concern for my so-called welfare ranges from the devoted to the nonchalant I'm very much afraid, not that I blame her, no, not in the least, no matter how intense and involved, this, which is to say I am no more than a job, an assignment to her, it would be foolish and even self-destructive to regard it in any other light.

"Can you grasp my hand?

I manage.

Even with my stiff left arm and hand I manage. But, no, not without a great deal of effort.

"And stand.

Can you stand for me?"

The same.

My right leg doing most of the work with the left just partially assisting in a precarious balancing act.

"Right, that's right. Now put your right arm around my shoulders. That's right."

Ah, but we make a hell of a couple.

I wonder if she guesses, realizes.

"Walk. All right? Let's take a little walk."

The nurse, Ms. Boyer has this inordinate faith in movement, it hardly matters where or for how long, no, she is firmly convinced that sheer movement of any sort will see me, us through somehow, whatever that may mean, the right, the good leg in front of the bad, the other which I somehow manage to drag behind, "See how simple? How easy?" a sort of an in joke between us, anything I find challenging, painful, practically impossible she simply terms simple and easy, she leads, guides, that is drags me into the corridor, "Full steam ahead," she encourages as though I were a ship on some transatlantic voyage, after a while I move as if on automatic pilot, one pain canceling another to leave me in a kind of feelingless limbo, we pass a number of rooms where she insists on stopping and glancing at the various occupants, "See," she asks triumphantly, "see? There are those worse off than you," she means both physically and emotionally although with her it's hard to say, "Ah, the humanity, " I try to kid, a lame joke to be sure although what other sort of option, of response does she leave me, and while sympathetic to the sufferings of others I am no more or less sympathetic than to those of my own, in other words the sufferings of others in no way mitigates or lessens my own, please, let's be clear, THE SUFFERINGS OF OTHERS NO WAY LESSENS ONE'S OWN, we plow ahead, at times I think Ms. Boyer quite capable of dragging me straight out of this hospital and into the well kept grounds that I occasionally think of as the other world, yes, if only I wouldn't expire, croak in the process, yes, Ms. Boyer out to kill or cure me I'm sure, whichever comes first, and it may be all the same to her, I'm not sure, but it may well be.

"Enough" I tell her.

'Just a bit more.'

"No! Enough!"

If I had the strength now I would seize her by the throat and throttle her, yes, she can tell by my voice and vicious stare, my body spent and shaking like a leaf, just what she means to accomplish by these little outings is anybody's guess, 'Hang on, hang on," she counsels, "we're almost home," meaning my cell, my prison, my final resting place before my final rest, I curse her under my breath, it provides the needed energy to complete the journey, I let myself fall into bed as if from a terrific height, "That wasn't so bad, was it?" she smiles, and it's all I can do to keep myself from flinging something at her, my clock, my glass of water or even my piss pot on the floor which I can hardly hope to reach, "You have no heart, Ms. Boyer," I manage to inform her, "a block of ice where your heart should be," and, "All's well, Mister Truman. You can continue with your dying if that's what you truly desire."

Near the end.

Or at the end itself.

I'm not sure.

But near the end one is faced with certain insurmountable difficulties, although challenges might be a better word, but certain contests of summation, of encompassing, grasping life as a whole, no, not life itself but one's own particular and unique existence, how over the years things have added up or simply failed to do so, ah, but what a lot of nonsense this is, when I was healthy or at any rate more or less functional this sort of thing never bothered me, my life, you see, let me repeat, MY LIFE, I instinctively understood that I could never seize, grasp it as though it were something accomplished instead of this perpetual movement from one moment to the next, and what was I after then, terrific question, let me repeat, WHAT WAS I AFTER, fancying myself some sort of composer with others simply playing along with this self-imposed definition, ah, people all too willing to humor you so long as you don't prove too great a challenge to their own notions of who and what they take themselves to be, but basically I worked, paid my taxes, loved, ah, yes, loved pretty much the same as everyone else, a few so-called unforgettable melodies and a handful of symphonies occasionally performed, no, I can't bear to think of those so-called successes and or failures just now, but how am or was I any different from any of the billions of my fellow creatures, yes, another terrific question, please, bear with me for a spell, I'm heading somewhere with this, I just might be, in other words in all my life what have I done but create one impossible situation or piece of music or even love after another, moved from one impossible situation or piece of music or love to the next, tell me you understand, and all this without ever having truly understood or challenged myself or anyone else around me, no, let's not white-wash, skim over this lightly at this late stage of the game, it simply won't do, and yet, ah, yes, AND YET what was there to understand, to challenge, have I not more or less followed my instincts, my so-called inner light, and, can, should one ask for anything more than this, please, I have a splitting headache just now, worked myself into a state with my mind just churning away for all it's worth, I ring the bell, Ms. Boyer off duty, it's one of the younger, sweeter nurses who in spite of their good intentions know nothing of my condition and appear quite incapable of making any sort of decision without consulting someone else, "A pill!" I yell at her, "Just give me a pill!" she doesn't understand of course, how could she, I've only managed to frighten her and make her run off in search of someone else, ah, in for it now I suppose, but to hell, really, to hell with them all, and to hell with me as well.

Just kidding.

Of course, I am.

I manage for the most part, indeed I do, and if not exactly a model patient I still harbor few if any misgivings about who and what and where I am, I am still perfectly capable of taking things lying down or standing up as the situations require, even now I only occasionally or periodically rock the boat as the saying goes, I lash out only when there seems to be no, absolutely no other way, let me repeat, ABSOLUTELY NO OTHER WAY, for instance, "Kill me or cure me!" I confronted Ms. Boyer the other day who very wisely did not bother to respond, she and I both realizing that there could be no response to such a guttural, instinctive outburst, in some ways my very helplessness an ally of sorts, it keeps me from taking myself, my situation, in fact life itself too seriously, although not always, no, certainly not always.

Yes.

"What's to become of me?" Samantha, my so-called wife, my last asked on her last visit.

Meaning?

No, I wasn't sure just what.

But she put the question in a sort of calm and meditative fashion, in other words not at all driven or in any way confrontational, and under the circumstances I could not help but feel for her just then, and this in spite of the fact that her concern for herself seemed to overshadow her concern for me, but, still, I could not bring myself to favor her with any sort of calming and or reassuring response, no, I simply could not.

"Do you understand?" she then insisted, "Do you have any notion what I'm talking about?'

It was a lovely sunlit day judging by the appearance of my room and the mild, the caressing breezes through the open window.

"My life, you see," she continued, "so tied up with yours, it occurred to me the other day, do you understand, Viktor, I mean do I now or have I ever had a life apart from yours, before I met you of course, but that was so long ago I can hardly recall, but since then it was you, all you I realized, you and your music and your friends, no, don't shake your head, don't bother denying it," I wasn't, my shaking my head simply an automatic reflex, "you pulled me in, Viktor, a helpless sharer in your life, but when, I'm quite serious, when did you ever share in mine? " she avoided my eyes during this little oration and stared into the distance out the window, "No, you didn't, you couldn't, of course, as I had no, you allowed me no life of my own," a little smile flickered across her lips just then as she momentarily glanced at me, "But this is not about blame, my darling, not at all, just a bit of sober reflection, but, really, what will I, what am I to do with myself once you disappear," a curious choice of a word, she could have said 'gone' or even 'dead' but she chose the milder, the more euphoric 'disappear,' "because I'm not ready, I'm sorry, Viktor, but I'm really not ready to disappear myself, you might be, I don't know, but at times you give every indication of being so, you no longer seem to give a damn about anyone or anything at all," and here again that slight smile flickering across her lips, "but the rest of us still have to manage, carry on somehow, and what will you have left me, how will you have prepared me for this, rooms full of unfinished scores, and, really, Viktor, what will I do with those, the faithful widow, the guardian of her husband's legacy," she pronounced 'legacy' as though it were an insulting, a four-letter word, "but, forgive me, Viktor, I don't know why I'm carrying on like this, I have no right, but it hasn't been a good day, not at all, on my way here I was nearly killed, sideswiped by a bus, I wasn't looking, my mind a million miles away, but forgive me, just uncertain and scared I guess, scared out of my wits if you want to know the truth."

So.

She put her head on the pillow next to mine then, 'Whose head? Whose pillow?' I asked myself, no matter, and softly, yes, ever so gently she started to cry, I didn't mind, a welcome respite from all the words, in fact after a while I began to feel quite comfortable just lying next to her, almost, and this will sound peculiar, but almost as if I hadn't a care in the world and she the same, as though it had all been talked and cried away, yes, I even shut my eyes and dozed off, I must have, because when I woke she, that is Samantha, was gone, and the nurse, Ms.. Boyer was taking my temperature, and, "You have no right, no, no right to treat others, especially the ones who love you the way you do," she looked down on me, but I had no idea, I swear it, no, absolutely no idea what she was talking about, let me repeat, ABSOLUTELY NO IDEA WHAT SHE WAS TALKING ABOUT, but it seemed useless to object, Samantha's so-called visit left me enervated, spent, and at any rate I hadn't the least desire to attempt to defend myself.

Is it all illusions in the end?

Or sometimes, often, always?

The mind playing tricks of course, more so now than ever before of course, although, no, I'm not at all sure of this, we spend much if not most of our lives trying to separate fact from fiction, yet how can we when fictions are all we have, all the mind is capable of creating, but don't mind me, it's just one of those days when I feel trapped like a fly in a bottle, seeing things but without the possibility of freeing myself, of breaking through the glass.

I spent a restless night.

Nothing unusual, at times I feel ill prepared to face the darkness, although darkness in a place like this far from an encompassing one which might be easier to deal with, I simply don't know, but so-called darkness in a place like this merely masquerading as, hinting at what I consider true darkness, certain lights out the window, the city in the distance of course, and then all along the corridors, the nurses, the doctors have to be able to navigate, to get to a particular room in case of an emergency, they're on perpetual guard and as long as there are guards there can't be anything re-sembling total darkness, still, a semblance of darkness to be sure, and when I'm ill prepared it's then that certain visions appear, present themselves as though I were a hapless, a defenseless victim, the very appearances easily assume the shapes and even personalities of people from my past, although, no, I can't exactly swear to this, recognition never complete, never entirely satisfactory, they may well be total strangers I had seen just once with no conscious recollection of my ever having done so, still, they do appear, what they want with me or I from them puzzling to say the least, some, yes, some attempt to embrace me while others rudely shove me away, all these fake dreams, because in the end they may be no more than those, out to test, to challenge or simply unnerve me it seems, some attempt to drag me to god knows what heights or depths while others appear only to make clear that they want nothing, ABSOLUTELY NOTHING to do with me, with and during these visions, for what else can I call them, time either races along or stands absolutely still, I hope you understand, TIME APPEARS TO STAND ABSOLUTELY STILL, it is quite useless to struggle or in any way interact with these entities, during these sleepless nights it's as though I lacked both the will and the power to assert myself in any way, in fact it's as if I didn't exist or existed as someone other than myself, just one more stranger among others, I hope that's clear, these visions, apparitions or whatever they may be carry with them the weight of all the things left undone in my life although they themselves appear as light as air, forgive me, I don't mean to dwell on things of this nature or on anything at all for that matter, I'm simply relating, conversing as it were, and, no, I'm after neither your sympathy nor your condemnation for any of this, they are no longer relevant to me, by now I feel myself quite beyond the boundaries of so-called normal existence, of any and all so-called appropriate behavior, just now I, we were simply considering illusions and or delusions, or light and darkness if you prefer, and in the end we have arrived exactly where we started, which is to say nowhere, do you understand, NOWHERE AT ALL, but we'll just drop it, let it go for now, really, there is nothing else to be done.

Situations arise.

Yes.

Even in a prison, a cell, in constricted quarters like this situations do arise.

Some, but not all, please, listen, NOT ALL having to do with the various machinations of the body, its unsettling manifestations of its irreversible decay, but NOT ALL, in fact I'm quite tired, annoyed at all the fuss made over changes in my temperature, blood pressure and irregular heartbeats, my headaches, my vertigo, my selective losses of memory, they're no one's business but my own as far as I'm concerned, in fact I wish nothing so much as to be left alone, do you understand, TO BE LEFT ALONE, "A man should be allowed to die in peace, don't you agree, Ms.

Boyer?" I once expressed to her, to which she, "Only if he lived in peace," snidely remarked, yes, something innately wicked if not entirely evil about that woman, no matter, but situations other than those having to do with my body do arise, in fact I'm often amazed at my latent but still present curiosity about things going on around me, none of them important of course or of any bearing on my so-called life, but the various comings and goings in this place with an inexplicable fascination for me, of other lives lived, contended and struggled with, yes, how is it that things continue the way they always have even though one longer feels a part of them, in fact, "Have you ever been in love, Ms. Boyer?" I once asked her point blank simply because I was curious or perhaps just meant to pass the time of day, but, no, she didn't reply of course, only stared at me for a spell to let me know that her private life had nothing, no, ABSOLUTELY NOTHING TO DO WITH ME, whereas my own physical and emotional life was there for everyone to rip apart, everyone but me that is, in the end, "I bet you tortured him and he you," I contented myself in remarking, at which she merely smiled, please, SHE ACTUALLY SMILED and nodded her head.

But in general, strictly in general situations do arise.

Yes.

And even a man in my condition, situation, someone for whom time is running out still finds himself very much caught up in time, how could he not, in the very predictability of his dying he is still occasionally fascinated by the unpredictability of the passage, the flow of time, his very thoughts, fears and remaining desires still made of time stuff, yes, I hope this much is clear at least.

Yes.

And even though less is more and more is less with all these situations, one is still forced to observe and to whatever slight degree participate, and that goes for the past as much as the present, yes, I just hope you understand, there is no exit until the final one, and in the meantime one is still forced TO PARTICIPATE, there is no getting around this I'm afraid.

Glimmers, yes, certain glimmers of clarity.
At times.
They come and go, appear and disappear like waves out to sea.

For example the other day, morning to be more precise, I recollected with what I can only term an overwhelming force that I was a composer once, not, as on other occasions, that I might have been one or a number of other things, no, there was absolutely no hesitation, no uncertainty in my mind, "I was a composer," I even said out loud, and with this single recollection others followed in its wake, any number of other recollections surrounding my having been a so-called composer.

Yes.

My various struggles, frustrations, failures as well as a number of my so-called successes, but for the most part I recalled my struggles, frustrations and failures more clearly than anything else, in fact it seemed to me that if I had become a composer, which I was quite certain that I had, it was mainly to embrace certain struggles and eventual failures, in other words from the very start I had set myself up to struggle and to fail, because of a certain amount of talent I had chosen music over other disciplines, but given other circumstances, other so-called gifts I could as easily have become a failed painter or writer or any other so-called creative person, the emphasis you see on my various failures and not on my so-called successes, in fact in the light of that morning's recollections I became convinced that any so-called creative person is doing nothing more than stepping back, stepping away from life itself, that, with the exceptions of few towering individuals, geniuses so-called, the ordinary creative person is nothing more than a coward who backs away from creating a meaningful and fulfilling life for himself and those around him and opts for an escape into his particular phony craft and artifice, someone who because of his peculiar combination of weakness and arrogance fools himself into thinking he is penetrating ever deeper into life while moving ever further away from it, yes, and then the recognition of this simple truth which under normal circumstances should have disturbed and upset me had, in my dying state, quite the opposite effect, in other words I embraced it much the way I had embraced all my other failures in life, 'I am my failures,' I even said to myself, and I just hope you see the simplicity, in fact the sheer beauty of such a rock bottom discovery, I AM MY FAILURES and not at all my so-called successes, and in some strange fashion this discovery or truth if you will, stayed with me, in fact buoyed me up for a spell, that is until my memories began to fade once more, the past once more blend with the present in their usual unrecognizable fashion, and once again I felt lost, yes, with no clear judgment as to who and what and even where I was, still, a lingering smile on my face as I shut my eyes, a smile I carried with me into my so-called dreams and visions, and that smile lasted, please, note, IT LASTED even if the reason for it was no longer evident to my mind.

"Yes. What is it you want?" Ms. Boyer asks.

And, "Everything and nothing," I reply.

It's a game I, we occasionally play.

I ring for her even though at the moment, no, nothing much is bothering me, physically and or emotionally, although such a statement is open to any number of contradictions, but let's just say for the sake of argument, I ring for her simply to have her enter my room, to watch her approach my bed, and eventually or perhaps right from the start she and I both realize that this is just a game we're playing, one of the few games we're capable of playing together, she towers over me, looks down, fixes me in her gaze, "Do you think I have nothing better to do with my time, Mister Probst, than to come running whenever you summon me?" she then asks, I stare back without blinking, something, yes, something passes between the two of us then, or any and all distances diminish for a spell, we, the two of us, keep still as if frozen in time for a spell, that is she standing and I lying, "There are others who need me," she says then, "others with more immediate, legitimate needs," but she makes no attempt to move, not just yet, the expression on her face neither kind nor unkind but fixed in a kind of permanence nearly impossible to read, "I was just wondering, Ms. Boyer. When will my eyes see the coming of the glory of the lord?" kidding of course, Ms. Boyer quite religious I suspect, although this is no more than a guess on my part, the thin gold cross around her neck may well be just for show, she appears to be on the verge of responding, of addressing the issue directly as it were, but, 'Is this the best you can come up with?" she asks in a monotone voice instead, I continue to stare, I have not yet given up trying to read what's behind the mask of her face, "Given time I can do better," I tell her then, the feeling nearly palpable then that we may be on our way to some sort of breakthrough in our communication, touch some sort of rock bottom reality both of us recognize, "A favor please, " I attempt, "What would it take for you to lie down next to me?" pushing things to an extreme of course, testing murky waters in which I'm sure to drown, her expression the same, please, note, HER EXPRESSION CHANGELESS, the result of my question is the following, we have moved beyond words, words between the two of us with built-in, definitive limitations, "You don't know me, Mister Probst," she says then, "and I sure as hell don't care to know you," curious, she rarely curses, rarely sabotages her calm, her efficient way with words, she leaves me no response, no comeback, an errant bee's insistent buzzing the only thing audible in the room for a spell, this time of year bees, flies occasionally mistake the open window for some grander opening, it takes a while for them to find their way back out, "You are wasting my time," Ms. Boyer finally announces, and without undo haste finds her way back out, much the way of bees and flies and other winged creatures.

Nothing fits.
Or everything does.
My myopic eyes no longer affording the clarity with which I mean to observe, to survey the things around me, I am better off shutting them, concentrating on my so-called inner visions, I see the lips, breasts, bellies, thighs of women I may or may not have known, the faces corresponding to the body parts not always easy fits, in other words recognitions of the ones no guarantees of recognitions of the others, the scents, the smells the same, although now and again I encounter some perfect fits, women about whose identities I harbor no doubts, please, note, NO DOUBTS AT ALL, they need little or no encouragement to gather around my bed and climb in beside me, 'Why have you kept me waiting so long?' I ask to which they respond with certain touches and strokes, we are or become a happy, a carefree bunch, 'All for one and one for all,' I smile which they understand perfectly, no possible misunderstandings as far as these particular visions are concerned, 'Ah, did or did we not have some terrific times back then' I sigh, or, 'Here we are, the same as we were back then,' we fit perfectly, flawlessly connected, 'Now you see me, now you don't,' I kid them and they me, I moan and groan in my bed, I can't help it, I only hope no one will intrude to question, to break the spell, it's the middle of the day or night,

either or, all of us beneath the blazing sun or the reticent moon, all of us open to suggestions, experimentations, nothing out of bounds, off limits, love in its myriad computations, manifestations, it is the morning after the night before or the night following the preceding day, stiffness of joints, arthritis, lumbago, psoriasis and varieties of lesions all forgotten, please, note IN THE PRESENT ALL THAT IN THE PAST, some inner rantings and ravings of course but I keep those to a minimum, with these visions I mean to disturb no one but myself, beneath my thin sheet I'm stretched wide across my bed, my movements remarkable, now fluid, now rhythmical but always, always graceful, please, note, ALWAYS GRACEFUL, 'You've been away too long,' one of the women whispers, actually a number of them do, it occurs to me then, I am making up for lost time before time is forever lost, cutting through all the red tape of dying, of time's inevitable demise, and then suddenly, out of nowhere a name appears, not just a body, a face but a name, Karen, an unquestionable identity, 'At last, at last,' I sigh, combined with the name her reddish hair and freckles leave absolutely no doubt in my mind, 'Ah, my one and only, my one true love,' I whisper, an out-and-out lie of course but what else but lies in visions, she understands completely, 'We made an amazing couple, don't you agree?' she even suggests, 'And still do!' I exclaim, but there is not a moment to lose, all our moments finite now and no longer infinite the way they once were, the dream, the vision slackens, I feel it slip from my grasp, 'Well, I must be off,' she tries to laugh it off, 'So soon, so soon?' vision time like any other time leaving a great deal to be desired, I try to mount her one last time, seek her treasure beneath her waist, 'Let go,' she gently pushes off, 'you must let go now,' I try my best to think of various terms of endearment but nothing, absolutely nothing comes to me, please, note, NOTHING COMES TO ME, chills and shivers as I open my eyes, the vision's moist heat turned to reality's cold sweat, I stare feelingless at the oppressive ceiling.

"What is it about the moon?" I ask Ms. Boyer who comes to check on me in the middle of the night. "And the clouds that occasionally hide it?"
No.
Let it go.

She is not interested, her concerns with the here and now, meaning this room, this patient and then the next and the next after that, she is far from willing to be distracted by anything as remote, as distant as the moon, in fact she doesn't even bother to look let alone gaze out the window, even though I'm almost certain, although this is just a feeling I have, that if she did bother to look and saw this clear, this waning moon with open eyes it would affect her in unpredictable ways or at the very least interrupt her trapping routine, and, then, yes, perhaps we could truly start to talk, the moon, yes, this particular moon as good a catalyst as I can think of just now, and I'm talking of its immediate perception as well as the memories it's bound to engender, personal, yes, of course, but also impersonal, the moon a terrific mirror, a repository of the very passage of time, eons of time in fact, ripped from the earth ages ago much the way, yes, much the way we appear to be ripped from others as well as ourselves, I try a different tack, the opposite approach, "Please, Ms. Boyer, don't look at the moon. Whatever you do, don't dare look at the moon," she doesn't of course, she continues with the reading of my chart and her highly efficient yet imper-sonal examination of my vitals, if I were already dead she would no doubt proceed in the very same fashion, in the process she now and again brings her face close to mine, all without touching of course, I become aware of a slight lemony scent I never noticed before, I'm tempted to remark on it but the uselessness of such a remark much stronger than the temptation, "Turn over, Mister Probst, and pull down your pajamas," she directs, she gives me a shot to either calm or excite me, I never know which, 'But I'm both calm and excited enough!' I mean to shout at her, 'By now you should know this better than anyone else,' she drags the night with her as she moves about the room, after a while I want nothing more than her disappearance in spite of an incomprehensible desperation to have her remain, "Do you flagellate yourself at midnight?" I ask as she finally prepares to leave, it's my last, my parting shot, she doesn't favor it with a reply, although, "Sleep well, sweet prince," she says before she shuts the door, not without a sense of humor, as cold as ice but not without a sense of humor to be sure.

Pathetic the number of tests performed on me.

They come in clusters, in waves, entire weeks go by without anyone bothering, and then others, other weeks when I'm constantly pulled, pushed, shoved, wheeled from one examination room, one machine to the next, it's as though someone had suddenly taken it into his or her mind to sustain my life for as long as possible, to take these so-called extreme measures, precautions, no rhyme or reason of course, I'd just as soon count myself among the dead as among the living, but, no, it's as though the preservation of life, please, note, THE SHEER PRESERVATION OF LIFE suddenly of utmost importance to those in charge, no doubt they prefer I expire somewhere else and in a manner that need not concern them in the least, the hospital's reputation at stake no doubt, in fact they would like nothing better than to have someone whisk me off to some unknown destination where I could get on with my private act of dying, but, no, I will not give them that comfort, that satisfaction, I intend to die in a manner and at a time and place of my own choosing, under their very noses if it pleases me, struggling, gasping for air while cursing my head off if it pleases me, no, yes, I will make them a present of my miserable death such as they have never received before, 'This, yes, this is death!' I will shout at them, let them truly see and appreciate as if for the very first time, let them be horrified and run off like mad into life, yes, that is my singular wish, the one legacy I intend to leave behind, yes, I fully intend to croak in a most unmannerly and insulting fashion, to leave them with something to think and talk about for the rest of their lives, 'Ah, but did you see how he refused to cross his arms, shut his eyes and quietly stop breathing?' yes, 'And what kind of man was this, must have been this to have clung to life with such unmitigated gall, such horrible abandon?' yes, no, I simply mean to set them an example to carry with them for the rest of their lives, my overwhelming passion for life translated into my utter resistance to death, let them make of it what they will so long as it explodes, destroys their sedate, their business-as-usual mentality, the hateful smugness of their so-called profession, I want nothing more or less than that.

But, please.

Don't mind me.

It's been a miserable afternoon, Wednesday if I'm not mistaken, although by now the names no longer significant, I reckon time simply by 'yesterdays,' 'todays,' and 'tomorrows,' all simplifications welcome near the end, at any rate a man in my condition entitled to certain rantings and ravings, they're of little or no consequence and may well be of some psychological benefit to the patient if not exactly those around him.

So, please.

Don't mind me.

Really.

In one ear and out the other if at all possible.

All visits, all visitors come as complete surprises to me.

Not entirely true of course, but true enough for practical purposes.

In fact, 'Who'll come next and when and why?' I frequently ask myself, just another of my many games.

Not that I ever look forward to any of these visits, these so-called visitors, I just as soon they visit someone else, pour their hearts out and torture someone else, someone still capable of appreciating such goings-on, I am no longer interested, too far gone for such nonsense.

Is that right?

"It's Samantha, your wife," I'm told.

The announcement, the introduction make me even more anxious about seeing her again.

A terrific looking woman.

Elegant, self-contained with a touch of class to be sure.

I both do and don't recognize her. Please, note, DO AND DON'T RECOGNIZE HER.

"Please, Viktor, don't stare at me like that."

She makes herself comfortable.

She adjusts her chair to make sure the angle of her vision includes both me in my bed as well as the world outside the open window.

"We met in spring," she muses. "I don't know if you recall but we met in springtime, Viktor."

I spy a spider crawling up a wall. Small, insignificant yet definitely visible.

She takes a deep breath that almost turns into a sigh. Nearly but not entirely.

"We met after a concert," she continues." " 'What an artist, what a genius,' I thought. I fell in love with your music before I ever fell in love with you."

I don't recall. Neither the concert nor our first meeting.

In fact I don't recall the particulars of any of my so-called concerts other than that they were unmitigated disasters, the music second rate of course, and the distance, ah, yes, the distance between the composer turned conductor always oppressive, was I ever anything other than a performing monkey with laughable abilities and talents to match, of course it takes so little to entertain, to please, people all too ready to surrender themselves to anything they think above their humdrum lives without realizing that their humdrum lives are merely mirrored by the so-called geniuses they applaud, but I don't know why I'm thinking of this now, it no longer matters, still, it's curious that I'M THINKING THIS NOW.

"Viktor, tell me. Have you ever loved me? I need to know. Tell me if you ever loved me."

All this without skipping a beat, without interrupting her gaze out the window.

To which I say nothing.

Please, note.

NOTHING AT ALL.

It's important to realize that even if I recalled, there can be no possible answer to a question like that, all possible answers to questions like that in the moment or not at all, and even then answers to questions like that highly suspect, questionable, but afterwards, no, more than suspect, more than questionable, useless and even destructive in fact.

She straightens her dress. Looks down, up and away.

At me then. A gaze as unflinching as she can manage.

"Serves me right for asking. Subject closed. Is there anything you need, Viktor?"

No doubt a rhetorical question, Samantha's, my so-called last wife's concern with other matters, yes, but how many others before her, no, not that it matters, but this, my so-called last wife, ready to dig, to explore with or without my assistance.

"Life, life and more life," I finally respond.

"What?"

"What I need. The only thing I need."

Her smile not entirely sincere, not entirely convincing.

Please.

It isn't that I don't sympathize with her.

I do.

I sympathize with everyone I have ever met and or known in my life.

I do.

That much clear at least, I hope.

"Please," Samantha picks up again, "tell me. Why must you be so hard on others, on yourself, no, that hasn't changed, not in the least, in fact I knew from the very start that you'd be a hard if not impossible man to love, but, no, I'm not blaming you, you and I both know that in the end we have no one to blame but ourselves, still, I'm asking you, Viktor, why this need to destroy even as you create, it's there, I never told you this, but it's there even in your music, your music soars even as it plunges, elevates as it depresses, and maybe, I'm just saying, but maybe this is what attracted me to it, and to you as well, this, your ability to elevate as well as to depress, we're all gluttons, suckers for punishment, Viktor, and I'm just beginning to realize, my darling, that you, yes, you were my ultimate punishment, and still are, no, please, don't stare at me like that, women are basically shallow creatures, perhaps we all are, but women basically seek their redemption as well as destruction in the ones they love, and, no, there was, there is no one like you to provide both, what you redeem with one hand you destroy with the other, and it's there, yes, there even in your music, which is why in the end people simply don't know what to make of it, even the ones who start out loving it simply don't know what to make of it in the end, you are the most wonderful man I've ever met but also the most frustrating, and lost, Viktor, lost to others as well as yourself, and it's not just now I'm talking about but always, your entire life, you were always the most frustrating and lost creature I've ever met."

And then she stops.

Abruptly.

And in the ensuing silence it's almost as though she becomes a different person, a person with nothing, yes, ABSOLUTELY NOTHING to do with the one who just raved and ranted, in fact in this enfolding silence I am no longer even sure she had said anything at all in the minutes preceding, please, realize, I'M JUST NOT SURE, in fact it's impossible to shake the feeling that during the preceding minutes she was anything but my mouthpiece, in other words that both the voice and words were mine and not hers at all, that between us, between my so-called last wife and me there exists and always existed nothing but this silence, the thoughts, the words all mine and not at all hers, that the only thing we ever truly shared, that ever truly belonged to both of us was this encompassing silence, and when I finally gaze at her as if for the very last time, and she the same, when she finally gazes at me as if for the very last time it's in and out of this silence we both gaze, words, both hers and mine, no longer exist if they ever have, and then this is how she leaves, she cannot, she dare not say another word, and I the same, I cannot, dare not say another word but simply watch her get up and leave.

Perhaps.

I'm just saying.

But perhaps my dying, my impending death not at all real, just a game I'm playing with others, with myself, in much the same way I've been playing games with others, with myself all of my life, and now my dying, my imminent death more or less, even exactly the same, do you understand, EXACTLY THE SAME, and this in spite of the obvious physical manifestations, my ever increasing fatigue and decreasing ability to focus, to remember, all a game I'm imposing on others, on myself.

Ridiculous.

Of course it is.

But I'm just saying.

There is merely this simple but often quite insistent need to make time pass, to entertain myself in some fashion or other, and, really, what better way than to make my mind wander and wonder, both I guess, but to make it wander now this way, now that, to give it free reign, to explore possibilities and impossibilities of the past as well as the present to attain some sort of final, absolute clarity or ultimate, definitive lunacy, yes, at times I would willingly embrace either, I'm almost sure I would.

One takes one's chances of course.

Please, listen.

In living as well as in dying what else but chances, no, not in death itself, in death all chances effectively destroyed, but while living and even dying the chances still remain, they're as real as the tumors within one's body or the sweat across one's brow, in fact I recently confronted Ms. Boyer, "Listen," I said, "please, listen to me. I fully intend to die a satisfying and happy death," she didn't understand of course, how could she have, and maybe I myself had only a vague notion of what I was talking about or even NONE AT ALL, as at all other times I may well have been kidding, fooling myself, no matter, I said what I said and that's where matters stood and still continue to stand.

Yes.

But what on earth could I have been talking about, could I have meant by a satisfying and happy death, at the very least that could have meant a satisfying and happy life, please, bear with me, and in all my life I have never met, known anyone who in some fashion led or accomplished what can be termed a satisfying and happy life, least of all someone like me, please, listen, all of us forever driven by unsatisfied drives, urges, by unattainable desires, by constant and tenacious fears of everything and nothing at all, please, note, EVERYTHING AND NOTHING AT ALL, life, our lives, we ourselves forever lacking any clear-cut goals, definitions, in fact any and all satisfactory explanations, our minds nothing more than breeding grounds for fake explanations that never correspond to actual reality, maggots that eventually dig, bore their way into the very fibers of our existence, but, no, I didn't mean to get started on this just now, I never do, it just happened or happens quite naturally or unnaturally as the case may be, and the sooner I desist the better off I am, or will be at any rate.

Please.

The other day or night, it might have been either, but let's not quibble, I had a dream, yes, an honest-to-goodness dream this time and not one of my numerous so-called visions, but an honest-to-goodness dream I vividly recalled afterwards, and I only hope this is of some slight interest to you, it may or may not be, but in this dream I was as if on trial, in other words in a courtroom of sorts and facing what I can only call my judges, no, I recognized none of them of course but they certainly seemed to recognize, to know me, in other words while they were strangers to me I was definitely no stranger to them, strange, I think you'll agree, but this was the unquestionable way of this dream, and they were there to either free or condemn me, yes, this much clear from the outset, but free me from what or condemn me to what, no, none of this immediately evident, at any rate I had to start, to begin explaining and defending myself, they asked no questions, you see, beneath their dignity somehow, it was all up to me, I simply had to start talking, and words, ah, here we go, I became all tangled up in my own words, let me repeat, ALL TANGLED UP IN MY OWN WORDS, in other words everything I was saying made little or no sense to me after a while, in fact absolutely no sense at all, I was sweating then in the dream, yes, much the way I'm sweating now, but, and this is curious, the fact that I was making no sense at all didn't seem to bother my judges, they simply continued to listen intently with every now and again a kind of a smile, yes, the briefest flash of a benign smile across their features, and the more they smiled the more emboldened I became in spouting my absolute nonsense, big mistake, the dream brief or long, no, that I couldn't recall, but in the end I was matter-of-factly condemned, 'Condemned to what?' I shouted, 'Why, to being who and what you are,' they graciously responded, they smiled and shook each others' hands, and then they simply left, that was it, you see, left the courtroom, the dream and me of course.

As I said, this may or may not be of any interest to you, but I'm simply relating the dream as it occurred, please, note, EXACTLY AS IT OCCURRED.

Just to pass the time.

Or for lack of anything better to do at the moment.

Which is a laugh of course.

It most certainly is.

Listen.

I am sitting cross-legged on the floor.

A terrific state of affairs and not without its heady sense of accomplishment, and if you asked, no, I could not possibly explain how I managed to bring it off, so, don't even bother, suffice it to say that it involved a lot of pain and trial and error, in fact when I started I had no idea what I was about to do, let alone why, all I knew was that I was simply sick and tired of just lying around or of being assisted, walked, carried, whatever from one corner of this room to the other, waiting, you see, yes, as if just waiting for something to happen, and I'm not strictly or solely talking of death now, not at all, but just waiting for SOMETHING TO HAPPEN, 'I'll show them,' I may even have thought but still without anything particular in mind, so then I started to move, everything crystallizing, becoming clear as I started to move, and, once again, I can't begin to describe the pain, the effort involved, I was doing nothing more or less than rebelling against the confining, the decrepit state of my body, every sinew, muscle, particle of flesh both inside and out causing me intense pain, let me repeat, every particle of me BOTH INSIDE AND OUT causing me intense pain, and yet I persisted, when I finally reached, landed on the floor I knew just what I had to do, I had to work myself into a sitting position, a cross-legged Buddha position, I just hope you appreciate the irony, the mocking incongruity of this, I who was never calm, collected and serene in my life now assumed a position that gave every indication of my being so, and against all odds I might add, and this, yes, this was the way I meant to be seen by whoever would walk into my room, whoever would discover me, 'oh, but I never knew he could be or actually was like this!' I even imagined him or her exclaiming, yes, heady stuff to be sure, and how long I originally meant to keep this up is anybody's guess, my challenge against my body, against others and perhaps even time itself, yes, I was even beginning to tell myself that now, yes, now I was beginning to feel no pain and with no, yes, ABSOLUTELY NO THOUGHTS in my head, an out-and-out lie, sheer nonsense of course, but I'm simply painting a picture, trying to show you the lengths I'm still capable of going to in deceiving myself.

So.

I'm sitting here cross-legged and more or less immobile, yes, credit where credit's due, and I don't know how much time has elapsed or will before I'll begin to shake, lose my balance and tilt over, no matter, the main thing is the moment, what I'm doing now, and even my so-called fakery doesn't bother me, no, not in the least, just part of the whole picture as far as I'm concerned, and whether someone actually does or doesn't come in, does or doesn't discover me, no, even that doesn't matter, what does matter is what I'm doing right now, sitting cross-legged like this on the floor right now, yes, the only thing that matters.

Nothing else.

"How does one prepare for death?"

Which is how I put it to Ms. Boyer the other day, taking her by surprise of course which was my full intention, in fact throughout interminable days and nights I often speculate, think about how best to accomplish this, to take her by surprise that is, not easy, something of a challenge to be sure, her mask nearly always on, her guard up, I'm simply saying, and by now she has learned to expect the unexpected from me, filed me away in the list of her more difficult patients, but that doesn't stop me, no, not in the least.

So.

"How does one prepare for death?" I asked her the other day.

Because she is something of a professional to be sure, well versed in dying and death, no question, and whom else to turn to, to consult with a question like this, you see my point, I'm sure, but my question not as simple as it sounds, my question with more of a psychological than strictly physical dimension, in fact even beyond the psychological if that makes any sense, hold on, I'll try to explain, a trick question, please, tell me you understand, but what I was asking Ms. Boyer, or rather what I was after was her admission that there was, there could be no possible answer to a question like this, that one could no more prepare for death than for life itself, I just hope you see where I was headed with this, but what I was really after was an admission of this sort on Ms. Boyer's part, a confession if you will that all preparations for death as well as for life are quite useless, perhaps even destructive in the end, they do nothing more than take our minds, our focus off some other all-important issue, you do understand, some other ALL-IMPORTANT ISSUE, but, no, don't ask what I mean by this as I'm not at all clear myself, but some other all-important issue one needs to constantly grapple with without the least hope of ever seizing let alone comprehending, no matter, but I was just hoping in this way, with her admission of unknowing that is, to make a kind of ally of Ms. Boyer or at the very least to establish a kind of link between us that because of circumstances and our very opposite natures never existed before, an exercise in futility I hasten to admit, but then name me one, yes, just a single thought or action that doesn't become an exercise in futility, no, I don't think you can, but my point, my only point is that occasionally I do try, no one can say I don't try from time to time, but, please, listen, after I raised this question, created this opening as it were, Ms. Boyer simply stared at me in her practiced, her usual fashion, a bit longer, a bit less accusingly than at others perhaps, but, still the fact remained, she stared at me in her USUAL FASHION, and of course this in no way diminished but simply reestablished or even reinforced the distance already existing between us, and, "Is that what's bothering you, Mister Probst?" she even asked and not without a certain degree of sarcasm as far as I could tell, and, "Yes, for the moment, yes!" I shouted at her, I may well have, but by then I was feeling little or no responsibility for my actions or reactions, after all a man in my condition, a dying man entitled to some leeway, to periodic outbursts no matter how unreasonable, and who knows but that it may even do him, if not necessarily others, some good, clear his congested cavities, his lungs, no matter, but, "Well, then, we're all right, aren't we, Mister Probst?" Ms. Boyer simply replied after a spell, and then she checked my vitals as usual, taking, yes, even taking a studied pleasure in this professional act, although given my heightened state of anxiety I may well have been mistaken in this, but, no, I don't think I was.

Fran.
Or Frances.
I'm not sure.
At any rate the name first and then the face, the image, no, that can't be right, let's just say the two as if appearing simultaneously which is unusual enough, but coming out of nowhere, of nothing which is more or less the way with me by now, from nothing something, you see, which makes me think of creation, the very beginning of time perhaps, ah, god help me, no matter, but Fran or Frances at any rate, a girl, a young woman with deep freckles and laughing eyes, can I say, think that, yes, I don't see why not, and reddish hair, yes, I may as well add, my first love I'm tempted

to say, please, listen, MY VERY FIRST, although after all this time I don't see how I can think, say that with any degree of certainty, no matter, something else of course, yes, there's always something else, in spite of the above mentioned attributes, if that's what they were, she wasn't particularly attractive, quite common, quite ordinary looking in fact, let me repeat, NOT PARTICULARLY ATTRACTIVE, but in spite or even because of this perhaps I loved her, yes, in fact loved with a passion bordering on, no, that's too much, let's just say I loved her the way any young man loves any young woman, and for the first time if I'm not mistaken, although given my current condition and the distance from the past to the present I don't see how I can recall anything with any degree of certainty, in other words what appears to be one way one time will no doubt appear another, no matter, I LOVED HER, in fact for a while my life seemed to revolve around hers and hers around mine, please, note, FOR A WHILE, and it was quite liberating, yes, the right word I think, but liberating to have no other care in the world except the one of loving someone and she you, bear with me, and this in spite of the fact that loving someone or so-called love also is or becomes a prison of sorts, in other words it masquerades as the whole picture when deep inside you know, are almost certain that it cannot possibly be the whole, the ENTIRE PICTURE, at any rate we were inseparable for a while, both of us quite convinced that the sun couldn't, wouldn't have risen or set without our thinking of one another, or that it simply wouldn't have mattered if it had, although in retrospect, please, note, IN RETROSPECT I'm quite convinced that it was nothing more or less than our mutual so-called sexual awakening, although now, yes, even now it breaks my heart to think, to say that, the truth of the matter is that no one has ever held me in her arms the way she had me, nor I her, that our sexual couplings whether in alleys, backs of cars, abandoned classrooms, WHEREVER were such as would, could never be repeated, and this in spite of the fact that SHE WAS NOT PARTICULARLY ATTRACTIVE as already mentioned, and if love is or was a prison then neither Fran or Frances nor I wanted anything more than to breathe, copulate and live in that prison, in fact I date my first so-called serious compositions from this time, although 'serious' a curious word as I doubt I have ever composed anything serious in my entire life, meant to of course, I always had but never with any degree of

SUCCESS, no matter, but we were talking of Fran or Frances just now and I would very much like to continue with it or her until I run out of steam or concentration or both, in other words until I grow sick and tired of the whole damned business, yes, can I just say the following, Fran or Frances was definitely the grand love of my life, please, note, the GRAND LOVE OF MY LIFE, and while I'm not sure what I mean or meant by that ,even now I'm glad to have said it, yes, with a hardened case like mine it's good to make such ridiculous, even outlandish statements from time to time, in fact I can think of nothing better to kill or cure me, and at this stage either would be welcome, I'm just saying, but either would be welcome I think.

Listen.
As long as I can keep my eyes open, as long as I can see.
No matter.
But the eyes extensions of the brain, yes, I must have read that some-where when I was still in the habit, or the ears, the nose, the tongue, take your pick, yes, all the various colors, tastes, smells, noises still available to me, within reason of course given the decaying, the unreasonable states of the mechanisms involved.
Here, I'll give an example.
Yes, just a single example should suffice.
A dog's barking.
Quite rhythmical, ordinary which makes me think the dog the same, in other words ABSOLUTELY NOTHING out of the ordinary, and I can't see him no, simply hear him from time to time through the open window, in other words his very appearance as well as his exact whereabouts open to question, the same for the reasons for his barking, tied down, perhaps, abandoned, open to question as well, I SIMPLY DON'T KNOW and probably never will, which makes his barkings all the more mysterious and, yes, exciting, I can and do hear him quite clearly of course, that is from time to time, but as for the rest I simply have to imagine, create him as it were, a lovely challenge to be sure, to my mind's eye he appears now one way, now another, and the same for the reasons for his barkings, they vary according to my moods, my inclinations, although the simple truth of the matter is no doubt more prosaic, this dog, this quite ordinary dog no doubt always

barks for the same exact and ORDINARY REASON, no matter, I only wish I could see, taste and smell as well as hear him, to see, you see, just to see how my imaginings correspond to actual reality, in fact hearing him is only a beginning of sorts, from hearing I want to proceed to all the other senses, to have my fill in other words and fully enter his life, yes, at times I feel that nothing, ABSOLUTELY NOTHING LESS will do, I only hope you understand what I'm talking about, but there is only the barking of course, sufficient but in no way completely satisfying, I just hope you see, his barking, while sufficient, is in no way COMPLETELY SATISFYING.

Listen.
Absence, yes, all absences significant.
I found this in my music of course, in fact I often thought and still do that my so-called music was made up of little more than absences, that throughout my so-called productive years I was aiming to create nothing more than the right sort of absences, in other words that the music itself was just a paltry excuse for trying to communicate the right sort of absences, without success I might add, important to note, without any NOTICEABLE DEGREE OF SUCCESS, yes, "But you're much too hard on yourself," I was often told, by whom, no, I can no longer recall, but let's just say that my so-called musical efforts had less to do with music per se than with ABSENCES, I want to make this absolutely clear, all the time I was composing my so-called music I was simply trying to create silences or ABSENCES if you will, in fact my entire life as a so-called composer con-sisted of nothing more than futile attempts at ABSENCES, failed efforts at various disappearing acts, yes, even then or especially then I wanted nothing more than to disappear from the world and it was through my limited talent, through my music that I meant to accomplish this, people misunderstood of course, PEOPLE ALWAYS MISUNDERSTAND, when they applauded they were fully convinced of applauding my so-called music and not at all my failed attempts at creating absences, silences, my very own absence in fact, and never, please, note, NEVER was I a greater fake than when I took my requisite bows, I deserved nothing, you see, yet somehow I managed to get something for my ridiculous charade, my masquerade, let me confess something, may I, all my life I looked for someone, anyone at all

to see through my ridiculous charade, my awful masquerade, to recognize me for the fake, the ABSOLUTE FAKE I was and still am, yes, that would have been something, a beginning of sorts , although of what sort I have no idea, still, I kept on composing and taking my bows, yes, this much must be obvious to you by now, the absences, the gaps, the silences forever eluding me, what I needed was a fresh, yes, an ABSOLUTELY FRESH START and still do, to start from zero, from scratch and firmly and consistently remain there, in other words no so-called progress of any sort but a total standing still, in other words a complete silence and death-defying absence, and then, yes, perhaps then I could truly start, really begin, but you must excuse me, I'm talking nonsense, sheer nonsense of course.

I'm telling you nothing you don't already know or at any rate suspect.

Nothing but sheer nonsense.

TO BE CONTINUED.

A lovely notion.

The perfect sign to hang above the bed of every dying patient in this way station masquerading as a hospital.

Or, ENTER AT YOUR OWN RISK.

That would do nicely as well.

Or, LEAVE AT YOUR OWN RISK.

Take your pick.

Or, and this is the last, promise, IT'S ALL BEEN A BIG MISTAKE.

Please, don't make me repeat.

Burn those signs into your memory and we're done.

Move on to something else.

My numerous accomplishments for example, those of the past as well as the present, yes, but for simplicity's sake let's just stick to the present, in fact I made a list, mental of course, but a kind of list the other day, here goes, scratching, coughing, burping, pissing, shitting, not necessarily in that order but the estimate fairly accurate, and while a reasonable person might well object that pissing and shitting don't belong with the other three mentioned, I decidedly object, they're more or less the same, in fact ENTIRELY THE SAME as far as I'm concerned, to distinguish among them would be a task beyond my current capacities, in fact, please, listen, at times they seem to occur simultaneously, in other words the scratching, coughing, burping, pissing and shitting as if a single accomplishment, the list goes on, I won't bother, suffice it to say they include a variety of other bodily functions, use your imagination, but none, you see, none of the mind, let me repeat, NONE OF THE MIND, and if you think we're back at the nagging mind-body problem, we're not, my present and only concern is with the physical and not at all the mental, I've had enough of the mental to last me a lifetime, and strangely enough even in my most so-called mental, so-called creative, composing days my focus at least as much on the physical as on the mental, in other words the very physicality of sitting down, leaning forward and putting pen to paper something I not only appreciated but actually looked forward to, the same with my hitting the piano keys, no, don't get me started, but the truth of the matter is I valued the very physicality of my so-called composing efforts much more than the actual music produced, so, this is not something entirely new, out of nowhere as it were, no, it's simply the continuation or full flowering of something already present in the past, the scratching, coughing, burping, pissing, shitting all make sense in the light of this, I don't see how they don't.

A cautionary tale somewhere in all of this, I just bet there is.

Given time it'll come to me, I don't see how it wouldn't.

Let's move on.

Signs, yes, return to the signs, pick up or continue where we started, ah, if only that were the case, in general I mean, that one could simply pick up, continue where and as one began, although, no, I don't think I'd wish that for anyone, no matter, but we were talking of signs, I have another, yes, let's just add one more to the list, LOSERS OF THE WORLD UNITE. YOU HAVE NOTHING TO LOSE BUT LIFE, or death, either or, and granted this sign a bit more complex, cumbersome than the others, still, I'm entitled I think, at this stage of my life, my dying,, I wish to leave nothing out, ABSOLUTELY NOTHING at all.

There.

We're done I think.

I just hope you appreciate.

A statement like that coming from me. I just hope you do.

We move on.

Did you think we wouldn't?

Ah, but how little you comprehend me or dying or my dying to be precise.

For the moment I'm feeling no pain, please, try to understand, to appreciate the unusual, the luxurious nature of this, you see pain, no, I don't know if I ever mentioned, made this ABSOLUTELY CLEAR, but pain is simply a given for me, my current state I'm talking about, in fact if no pain then no sight, hearing, tasting, smelling, whatever, and no thinking of course, please, ABSOLUTELY NO THINKING at all, please, I'm simply trying to clarify matters, to point out how things actually are, but pain the given, the mode, the method, the catalyst or the sine quo non if you will, there, enough I think, but for the moment there is none, and while not asserting that this makes for a greater ease or even clarity of perception as I'm no doubt all drugged up, I'm simply pointing out the unusual, the welcome nature of it.

An accompanying danger of course if one identifies death with the absence of all pain, but, no, neither pain nor death just yet, I think I'm making this sufficiently clear.

All in all a marvelous state of affairs, if I can use such an extreme and suggestive description.

Ms. Boyer watching me with a great deal of curiosity, even awe perhaps.

Some kind of experimental drug perhaps.

No, yes, I wouldn't put it past her.

As a matter of fact everyone here an expert at experimenting, trying different approaches both MENTAL AND PHYSICAL at easing one's last, one's final journey, that's a laugh, if they're so interested they should simply undertake the journey themselves, which of course sooner or later they all will, but I'm getting sidetracked, thing is, part of me wishes they wouldn't, stop their infernal interference with what I often regard as THE NATURAL COURSE OF EVENTS, in fact, "Stop making such a fuss, Ms. Boyer," I told her the other day, not that she ever does, I mean she both does and doesn't, but that's exactly what I told her simply to get a rise or observe her reaction, ah, if only I could, at times I think that EVERYTHING WOULD BE ALL RIGHT if only I could get a rise out of Ms. Boyer, my last best hope I often think, no rhyme or reason, I just do, in fact, 'Charm Ms. Boyer and you'll charm death itself,' I tell myself, yes, I don't know if I ever told you but in spite of all my obvious shortcomings in life no one ever accused me of not being charming, quite the opposite in fact 'Ah, what a charming man, lover, composer or whatever,' yes, that was the general refrain, yes, in fact if there is anything in this so-called life of mine that makes it hang together, which it never did of course but let's just say for argument' s sake, if there ever was it's this persistent CHARM OF MINE which I could turn on at will, in other words as the situation required, and I still might, that's the thing, you see, everything withstanding, I still might.

Overworked of course.

Ms. Boyer I'm talking about.

Yes, that's the simplest explanation by far for her resistance to my so-called charms, for my annoying inability to bring her out of herself as it were, although god only knows what I would then find there, what I would be confronted with, but that's not the issue, NOT THE ISSUE AT ALL as far as I'm concerned.

"Open wide."

Yes.

Even in my heightened or lessened or whatever state of awareness, in other words in my temporary painless state of awareness it's business as usual, Ms. Boyer simply carries on the way she always has and no doubt will till the end of time or my death, whichever comes first.

"Such cold hands."

Or warm.

I forget which.

"Turn over."

My compliance something to behold.

Have I always been this compliant, sometimes, often, never, I only wish I knew; the past the past and the present something entirely different, in other words who I was or may have been in the past open to question, not that it isn't now, in other words who I am or may be in the present, I just hope THAT'S CLEAR, we're talking of two entirely separate, different entities and the nature of both, yes, I think that's correct, open to question.

Wasting time.

Please.

But pain or no pain, clear or blurred vision, I'm simply wasting my time.

I just hope that's clear.

Have I always?

Often, sometimes, never?

Please.

In retrospect, follow if you can, but in retrospect it seems I have always wasted my time, my entire life, please, note, MY ENTIRE LIFE consisting of nothing but various acts, activities of wasting time, or perhaps of just one composite, ONE GIANT ACT of wasting my time, and in this I include all my activities, my various so-called achievements, my numerous liaisons no less than my questionable musical achievements, the two somehow related in my mind, in other words my failed love affairs intricately linked to or no more than extensions of my failed musical accomplishments or the other way around, and the two, pay attention, but the two may well be reduced to or summed up by this single overriding and or all-important question, HAVE I EVER TRULY LOVED ANYTHING OR ANYONE IN MY LIFE, in other words have I ever been truly committed to or been passionate about anyone or anything in my life beyond the narrow concerns of the self, no, I'm not playing any games just now or perhaps my last, my final, my ultimate game, I mean who's to say, but you may simply consider this a rhetorical question if that makes it more palatable, I wouldn't mind, no, I most certainly would not.

Please.

All approaches, questions, doubts ridiculous in the end.

Poor old Rene.

Descartes I mean.

'The only thing we can't doubt is that there is doubting.'

Poor old bastard.

Yes.

And once again one of my splitting headaches, my temporary reprieve of a relatively short duration it seems, you see how nothing works

in the end, let me repeat, NOTHING WORKS IN THE END, but I take full
blame this time, shoulder all the burdens I'm still capable of supporting.

I don't see how I can avoid it.

"Everything all right, Mister Probst?"

I reply nothing.

My voice silent, my lips firmly sealed.

Let her make of it what she will.

Yes.

One's no one's fool in the end.

That would be nice I think.

Or one becomes everyone's fool including one's own.

Equally true I think.

Talk about your cautionary tales.

I don't recognize the woman visiting me, or perhaps I simply don't
wish to. Simpler, easier this way.

"I waited, hesitated for the longest time before coming to see you.
You know how it is."

No. I don't." Absolutely no idea.

"But then it came to me, a feeling, an inspiration, 'Why not visit,' after
all, the past is the past and as long as I had no intention of resurrecting, of
dwelling on it, a visit would be all right, we're no longer connected, neither
of us capable of harming the other.'

I shut my eyes.

The better to hear.

Or not.

Easier to hear with my eyes shut.

Or not.

"I don't know if you remember. I do, of course, as though it were
yesterday. Our passionate, terrible, destructive affair, are all affairs destructive you think, no, don't bother to reply, you needn't trouble yourself, but
everything about our affair as clear as the present moment, in fact as though
it were happening now, right now and not six years ago, please, you needn't
turn away, I'm not here to make trouble for either of us, I no longer have
the will let alone the energy, the strength, this is just a simple visit, my

darling, something I felt I owed you as well as myself, it's not every day after all that someone, some someone who was such an intricate part of my life is about to take his final bow, I hope I'm not upsetting you, not at all my intention, but you see how things stand or stood or still do with me, no, you needn't bother making faces, I'm simply thinking out loud, but look at me, really, by now I'm an old hag myself, and if not an old hag then someone who certainly had her share of suffering, looking and feeling the way I do I'm certainly no longer a danger to anyone, least of all you, what's the expression, 'Water under the bridge, ' well, it's not just water so much as a regular deluge, the winter snows all melted and come rushing down, listen to me, you'd think I was still a writer, a working poet, you needn't worry, no more inspiration, no more words for years now, for now I'm simply surviving, stretching things out the best I can, you the same I expect, but we were talking of the two of us, of all we meant to each other way back when, how I swore that you were driving me crazy and you, no, I don't think you said much of anything at all, you were simply satisfied to let everything run its course, for time to undo what it foolishly started, let me just ask you this though, were or weren't we desperately in love, at one time I mean, I need to know, that's not asking too much after all these years, no, not even a nod of the head, that's all right, you're still the same and always will be, but by now all wounds are healed, look at me, you no longer have the power to inflict new ones, and the tables are turned I suppose, do you remember when you came to visit me in the hospital just the way I'm visiting you now, 'Foolish, foolish woman, ' you said, I remember the exact words, and my wrists all bandaged up because I had cut both to try to make sure, but there I was and there you, much if not exactly the same as you are now, surely there must be some sort of irony to all this, and was I glad to see you, I mean back then, no, about the same as you are glad to see me now, you see by then it was all over for me, at least that's what I told myself, 'Get out! Get out!' I even shouted at you, that's the way I remember it, although I couldn't have, too weak from the loss of blood, just whispering, hissing perhaps, 'Get out,' do you remember, but inside, you see, inside I was def-initely shouting, still am from time to time, no, no, you needn't worry, I'm on my best hospital behavior as you were back then, but I must say you're looking extremely well in a terrible sort of way, that's funny, right, you used to appreciate my jokes almost as much as I appreciated yours, but I don't regret having come, I simply had to, and although you refuse to open your eyes, even that's all right with me, I just hope you realize, by now everything's all right with me, and I didn't bring you any flowers, just the way you didn't when you visited me, in too much of a hurry to get there I suppose, but with me it was just the opposite,

I was in no hurry at all to see you, I simply walked, ambled my way over here, 'Oh, is this where I'm going', I even remarked to myself, but I brought you no flowers, no, nothing at ·all, I just didn't think it appropriate."

And long after she's gone.

Or shortly.

I still have no idea who she is, please, I want to make this absolutely clear.

NO IDEA WHO SHE IS.

It might help if I did, maybe not, truth is I just don't know.

'   "Seems like a nice woman."

Listening all this time?

I wouldn't put it past Ms. Boyer.

I piss in my bed.

A delicious feeling, total satisfaction.

Give her something to do besides spy on her patients.

Everything coming up roses.

Can I think, say that?

I don't see why not.

But someone left me a dozen roses the other day, blood red to be sure, but I must have been fast asleep, well out of it, when I came to, reentered, returned, only the roses were left, ah, if only every visit were the same, nothing but some meaningless gift, some ridiculous memento to mark its passing, flowers both meaningless and ridiculous of course, all flowers brought to patients in hospitals both meaningless and ridiculous as far as I'm concerned, and roses, especially red ones more than any and all others, not that I have anything against flowers in the wild or even in flower shops, quite the opposite, in fact the other day I clearly or almost clearly recalled my carrying a bunch in my arms, rushing to see someone with a bunch of flowers in my arms, the image quite vivid, as a matter of fact I could nearly reach out and touch the flowers, touch myself in the past, yes, let's just say I had to stop myself from reaching out to touch the flowers, to touch myself in the past, now how's that for a mental adventure, the intended recipient a blur, as good as nonexistent, only the flowers, please, note, only the FLOWERS in sharp focus, and they had been roses, blood red in fact, quite a coincidence, it most certainly is, but in my present state and or condition I want nothing to do with flowers, no, ABSOLUTELY NOTHING AT ALL, flowers for the dying a total waste, or worse, the ultimate insult, bringing life into a place like this, whether symbolic or real entirely beside the point, but in the case of flowers all too real, I trust you agree, GLARINGLY, EVEN PAINFULLY REAL, after my final disappearing act, my definitive departure, they, whoever they may be, can bring all the flowers they want to my so-called funeral, I will be well out of it by then to care one way or the other, to express any sort of gratitude or mockery, derision, by now you must realize I'm quite capable of both, even in a single breath, simultaneously as it were, but let them come with their carefully or haphazardly selected flowers after I'm gone, even roses if that's their preference, and blood red to boot, although white or at any rate pale roses more appropriate for the dead, no matter, by then I'll be in no position to care, yes, that's the thing, the problem I think, in the past as well as or especially in the present, one sometimes, often or perhaps even always falls into the TRAP OF CARING, and the sooner I'm done with it, for good I mean, the better for all concerned, caring nothing but a disease, the ultimate weakness, please, don't interrupt, I've given this a great deal of thought, start to care and you're as good as dead, yes, even WORSE THAN DEAD perhaps, on the other hand how else to go through life than TO CARE FOR EVERYONE AND EVERYTHING IN SIGHT, I just hope I'm making myself clear, the gist, the very crux of the matter, in other words throughout my entire life have I or have I not been a so-called caring individual, no, it's impossible to answer a question like this, I won't even try, but here's my point, the only point I set out to make, flowers after I'm dead and gone but not before, yes, I can even see them tossed on my coffin as it's lowered into the ground, yes, farewell and good riddance yes, that's my point, and not a dry eye at the cemetery or the opposite, no one willing or capable of shedding even a single tear, all right either way, I'll be beyond their clutches by then, and my own I hasten to add, yes, especially my own, untouched and untouching, oh, but what a marvelous, what a terrible prospect, I can't make up my mind, no, I simply can't.

Leave it to me.

To make a simple issue complicated, living and or life complicated, dying and or death complicated.

Yes.

Leave it to me.

Drive myself quite crazy in the end if I'm not careful.

I held her in my arms.

Yes, let's just say.

Someone, someone, someone, somewhere, somewhere, somewhere, something, something, something.

But I held her in my arms, let's just say.

And oh, what a time we had, yes, I think I can say that, even if not safely, but how it all came together then, or we, yes, how WE CAME TOGETHER THEN, and this, yes, this in spite of the particular circumstances surrounding that particular time, place as well as the people involved, in other words the TWO OF US, but that she was the GRAND LOVE OF MY LIFE I have no doubt, and I hers perhaps, please, note, PERHAPS, ah, that particular connective will be the death of me yet, or all things subjunctive if I may be so bold as to suggest, all things subjunctive will be the death of me yet, let's move on, I held her in my arms, yes, that's how we started, and then the rest, whatever the rest was or may have been, the GRAND LOVE OF MY LIFE I think I just said, asserted although not without a certain amount of doubt allowed to creep in, we moved beneath the stars, the moon or even the sun perhaps, yes, more than likely it was one or the other but I'm not excluding the possibility of its having been all three, in other words night or day, it seems to have made little or no difference, that is as far as our joint movements were concerned, in other words in, through, above, below and next to one another, clear enough I think, in other words the physical, the varieties of physical movements I'm talking about but not, please, note, NOT without a certain corresponding to the so-called mental, emotional, spiritual or what you will, yes, I'm almost sure, as a matter of fact, "I love you, Cynthia," or Sylvia or Gloria or perhaps Eve I even said, I'm pretty sure, after all was or wasn't she the GRAND LOVE OF MY LIFE, I'll leave that for you to grapple with, in my present weakened state it's just too much for me to tackle, some other time perhaps, ah, but just listen to me going on and on about time, as though I weren't running out of it, any month, week, day or even hour perhaps, no matter, but here, yes, here is or was the fly in the ointment, to my half or even full-hearted confession, comment and or interjection she simply responded and or remarked, "I just want to fuck," please, note the frank brutality and or painful sincerity of such a statement, I most certainly did, I mean calling a spade a spade at a time like that highly misplaced, inappropriate and perhaps even destructive, yes, but that may well have been the very reason I loved her, or one of them at any rate, please, consider, I JUST WANT TO FUCK may well have been the most guileless, direct and even sincere outburst to sum things up, I'm not denying, but still, if she was the GRAND LOVE OF MY LIFE what was I to say, to do, in other words how to continue after that, but continue I did, no question, and perhaps even with a renewed dedication, ah, the vigor, the vitality, the sheer abandon of youth, I mean if that's what it was, and it will never be like that again, I would bet my remaining months, weeks, days or hours on it, no, NEVER LIKE THAT AGAIN.

I just hope that's clear.

Yes. No.

It'll never get any clearer than this, I assure you.

Beethoven. Mahler.

Yes, let's just proceed in this fashion, others, yes, any number of others of course, but for some reason my lumbago, recurrent I assure you, makes me want to turn to music, not my own, god help me, but those of Beethoven and Mahler, just two of the greats that popped into my mind, yes, 'Beethoven help me,' and, 'Mahler help me,' I was even thinking just now, as if anyone or anything could, please, note, I'M BEYOND ALL HELP BY NOW, but let's just hypothesize, not entirely illegitimate for a man in my condition, so, if anyone or anything could help me just now it would be certainly Beethoven and Mahler, or certainly the music of Beethoven and Mahler.

Not that I'm ready to listen to either of those, far from it, they would simply disturb, upset and perhaps even explode my already exploding universe, yes, just one explosion at a time if you please, my last, my final, my definitive explosion to be precise, but throughout my so-called life, musical and otherwise, it had always been Beethoven and later Mahler to cure me of my various psychoses, neuroses or just plain melancholia, although nothing plain about melancholia I assure you, in other words Beethoven delivered when nothing and no one else would, and later Mahler the same, which is not to say that I idolized them in any way, yes, the thing about me was always this total lack of idolizing anyone or anything at all, please note, even at the height of my so-called fascination, my intoxication with Beethoven and then Mahler I could just as soon leave as take them, I'm only slightly, somewhat exaggerating, but while both Beethoven and Mahler meant the world to me at one time, and still, yes, they still do, I was and still am perfectly capable of seeing through their shenanigans, in other words neither Beethoven nor Mahler particularly skilled at what one can only describe as THE CONDUCT OF THEIR LIVES, and in this they definitely resembled me, to a tee you might say, but not, of course not in their music, their music something of an ultimate, something of a standard against which I once dared to measure myself or something to which I once foolishly aspired, in fact I might have never begun composing or even thinking of music in a serious way, as a sort of ultimate redemption or damnation, had it not been for the music of Beethoven and later Mahler, the irony, of course, is that from the start, please note, FROM THE VERY START, I realized that I could, would never approach let alone duplicate the achievements of a Beethoven or a Mahler, in other words listening to the music of Beethoven and later Mahler while disclosing certain immense, certain unparalleled possibilities also had the dubious, the undesired effect of making me realize my then current and no doubt future limitations, in other words from the very start the music of both Beethoven and Mahler at once elevated as well as crushed my spirit, set me to exploring in other words while guaranteeing that all my so called explorations would end in utter failure, as nearly all undertakings in life are bound to end in UTTER

FAILURE, a valuable if disheartening lesson to be sure, in other words with both Beethoven and Mahler I touched the zenith as well as the nadir of all my hopes and expectations, and, as already mentioned, it's ironical that in the end it wasn't my music but my VERY LIFE to resemble theirs, in other words my personal failures in some ways mirroring theirs while my so-called musical successes not even approaching let alone duplicating theirs, no, you have to be born a genius to rise, to soar above the mundane, the destructive and ultimately self-defeating, in music I'm talking about, and how many geniuses like that exist or have ever existed, no, in some ways I've inherited all their failures and none of their successes, mind you, I'm not complaining but simply observing, in fact I cannot envision my life, my so-called past without this drive, this false hope of someday achieving what either Beethoven or Mahler have, ridiculous, absurd, I know, but it's just such ridiculousness, such absurdities that make one survive, carry on from one day to the next, and when that's gone, please, listen, then everything else is gone as well, in other words ALL IS LOST in the end, I'm just saying, all the same the fact remains that right now, at this precise moment I would like to do nothing so much as to listen to the music of either Beethoven or Mahler, that is I both would and wouldn't, imbibe as well as reject them, it's a monstrous state of affairs, I'm sure you agree, to want something so desperately while wholeheartedly rejecting it at the same time, but I'm beginning to annoy if not necessarily bore myself, no, I could never bore myself while thinking of either Beethoven or Mahler, but annoy myself for sure, yes, better stop, best to stop just now.

Sometimes.
What?
Just sometimes.
What?
I'll go on.
Hair, forehead, eyes, cheeks, nose, lips.
I'll go on.
Terrific the way one can carry on, continue at times.
Not always.
Just sometimes.

While at others, yes, everything just a blur, the eyes have it over everything else, inner as well as outer I'm talking about, a certain clarity of vision followed by what, darkness, EVERYTHING GOING DARK, I just hope you appreciate, not a moment to lose with everything about to be lost, yes, I think I can safely say, although all setbacks merely temporary perhaps until the last, the final one, but here, here is what I told myself the other day, 'Her eyes were like emeralds,' yes, or like the sea with its brilliant transparence, and then, yes, how she touched herself down there, or I perhaps, in this business of memory possibilities frequently arise only to be negated later on, soon, soon, soon you tell yourself but then the soon doesn't come, it NEVER MATERAILIZES, other things materialize, please, note, other things DO MATERIALIZE, but not that one, that particular, that sought for thing, what ever it may be, and too bad, yes, just too bad for memory, for thinking in general, and lest you think there are ways of creating or affecting different approaches, no, THINK AGAIN, which is what we do, basically I mean, thinking, remembering things over and over again but never or hardly ever the RIGHT THINGS, please, let's just be clear about this one thing, HARDLY EVER THE RIGHT THINGS.

No matter.

We'll get back.

Promise.

I'll do my best.

Where were we?

Eyes, forehead, cheeks, breasts, thighs.

All or none of the above.

All I think.

Ah, but how I wandered and or wondered across her body like some explorer across a once familiar and unfamiliar landscape, and as an explorer I held my own I think, and hers as well of course, I wish, yes, I only wish that I could report my having reached my destination, my goal, in fact THE PROMISED LAND if you prefer, yes, but no matter how much I'll go on about her throat, chest, groins, yes, especially HER GROINS, I'll come up short, in other words memory and or reality is bound to come up short, throw in any number of anatomical parts for good measure and the result will still be the same, and, I'm just saying, but if you think some kind of comparison might be of some help, no, it absolutely won't, in other words all attempts DOOMED TO END IN FAILURE, and this from the very start I'm talking about, hardly worthwhile to begin, to continue, and yet, and yet.

No.

I don't know.

I simply don't.

We sit and talk.

Is that right?

Ms. Boyer and I.

She in her chair, or a chair to be precise, and I in my bed, or a bed to be precise.

Yes.

Sitting upright in my bed, which under the circumstances is no small, no mean accomplishment, not one of my better days let's just say, in fact a dizziness that enfolds and nearly overwhelms, let it go, ah, but how one struggles against all odds at times or no longer simply gives a damn, yes, I think that's right, but, still, Ms. Boyer and I having a kind, some sort of conversation, A CONVERSATION, although conversation might be a bit of an exaggeration, let's just say that from time to time one of us says something and the other listens, more or less I mean, or the other says something and the one listens, it sounds complicated but, trust me, it's anything but, as a matter of fact silences abound, let me repeat, SILENCES ABOUND, as a matter of fact if it can be asserted that there may be conversations above, below as well as in and through silences then that is exactly what is taking place, with now and again a few words tossed in, it stands to reason, a few words from time to time.

If it sounds like I'm beating around the bush, I'm not.

Trust me.

The last thing on my mind.

We'll continue.

That is she and I continue.

"Make a fist."

What?

Still possible?

Ah, but in the past, the distant as well as the recent past, I just don't know, fists, all sorts of fists, I could close, open, then close my hands without any noticeable strain, any effort, grab, grasp now one thing, now another and another after that, but back to the present, the fistless present, I have little or no choice, and even my success, after a while and in a manner of speaking, only a reminder of my real, true, effortless successes in the past, my SUCCESSFUL FISTS of the past, but we move on, it's remarkable how I, we always manage to move on.

What else?

Through our words and silences, although more hers than mine, I hope that's clear, but through words and silences I desperately try to catch glimpses of what I can only call the real, the genuine Ms. Boyer, not easy, I assure you, in fact it brings a smile to my lips how difficult, how impossible it seems, I hesitate, what else, in the midst of words, of silences I frequently hesitate, WHAT ELSE, it would be simpler just to cease and desist, with everything I'm talking about, but just to CEASE AND DESIST, the scene in my hospital room only now and again clear to my head, for the rest it's blurred or just a blur if you prefer, still, please, note, STILL at one point I call her "Anne," or, "Anna," I'm not sure which, but, BUT I'm not sure of the audibility of that name, either one, in other words does or doesn't my voice carry sufficiently for her to hear, she gives no clear indication, 'Anne' or 'Anna' as if lost in some kind of void which my voice isn't strong enough to penetrate, let's move on, but what a breakthrough if my voice actually managed, to penetrate the void that is, and then, oh, yes, then it would be all up to her, I can't emphasize this enough, ALL UP TO HER after that, our relationship based on a new or at any rate different footing, and this without any certainty of just what I mean by this, but, here we go, she just might respond by calling me 'Viktor,' and then, what else, really, WHAT ELSE, I don't know, but it would be a beginning of sorts, you see my point, in the midst of this prolonged but definitive ending a beginning out of the clear blue, OUT OF NOWHERE as it were, but let's not get ahead of ourselves, a man in my condition has to steer clear of all false hopes, of hope in general, nothing worse than hope in a hopeless situation, I'm just saying, but one can't be too careful, no, a man in my condition can't be too careful about something as dangerous as hope.

Enough.

The beach, the ocean, the setting sun.
How?
My eyes shut.
And when I open them?
No, nothing after I open them.
Any objections?
Sometimes, let's just say, yes, sometimes.

Certain promising images or visions if you prefer, ah, but we've been through all this before, I'm sure we have, if not one image or vision then another, I seem to have no control over them, let me repeat, ABSOLUTELY NO CONTROL over them, they may be all the same or different, even that's not entirely clear, and then a woman needless to say, but some woman or other who appears to scatter herself across the waves, the sand, just follow if you can, but let me tell you something else, my so-called images or visions filled with impostors, women who may have been real once but no longer are, or perhaps they never were, please, just give me some credit for trying to get to the bottom, the ABSOLUTE TRUTH of things, some of the women ill-bred, quite common while others with something of an unattainable elegance, ah, if only I could squeeze them into one, just a single TIMELESS WOMAN, yes, I'm sure. I could be done with it, with her once and for all, please, just imagine the possibility, TO BE DONE WITH EVERYTHING at once, just one big fun house of memories gone haywire SUDDENLY ENDED, let me repeat, no visions, no memories, no perceptions, and these of the past as well as the present I'm talking about, no more struggles, contentions with their ensuing interpretations, and painful, yes, I needn't add, imagine a tunnel, yes, an endless tunnel with no possible light at the end, yes, that's precisely what I'm talking about, the ridiculous blending into the sublime or the other way around but with both, that's correct, both exploding into nothingness, or a kind of an in-joke that becomes, what, NOTHINGNESS in the end, no more erratic heartbeats, uneven breaths, uncertain touches, in other words back, back, BACK to a time before time ever grasped, ever seized me, TIMELESSNESS in other words, I just hope this isn't too much for you, in my decrepit state this unfortunate tendency to pile it on, exaggeration the antidote to visions with diminishing returns, or let me yes, all I want is to see this one single thing with an unmatched clarity, in the past I mean, yes, that would suffice I think, because then, then, THEN I might see a similar image or event with an equal clarity in the present as well, please, just realize the importance of what I'm saying, AS IN THE PAST SO IN THE PRESENT, or something, yes, definitely something along those lines, please, if you think it's easy to come up with such a simple formulation, calculation, it's not, far from it, it's taken me I don't know how many hours, days, weeks, months to come up with it, but what matters now is that I actually have, in other words if SUCH AND SUCH THEN SUCH AND SUCH, the gist of my argument, my discovery, and for the moment I'm satisfied, although who knows what other formulation and or discovery I'll come up with tomorrow or the day after or the day after that, to subvert, to cancel this seemingly all important one, no matter, the main thing is I'm satisfied for now, yes, I don't see how anything else matters.

Samantha.
My so-called wife, my last.
'Are you all right? Please, just tell me. Tell me you're all right."
Finders keepers.
Yes, as far as words are concerned.
And for the moment I wish neither to find nor to keep them.
May I say something?
No, not loud enough to be heard, I have neither the voice nor the inclination, just whisper it then, addressing no one but myself.
"Nothing works."
You understand?
Not a blessed, not a damned thing.
"What's that?"
I repeat nothing.
All my life nothing but repeats, repetitions and I'm not about just say the following, difficulties abound, bound to abound in the end, in other words it's damned if you do and damned if you don't, I think you know what I'm talking about, I just hope you do.

But we were on the beach just now with the rising or setting sun.

I'm not particular.

And the ocean with its calm or disturbed, if ever so slightly, waters, I'll take what I can get, and in the distance or near a woman, approaching not receding, please, note, NOT RECEDING, gloriously naked, and in time and with time it's nothing but a question of time, let me repeat, nothing but a QUESTION OF TIME, although at this stage, with this vision I'm merely guessing, ah, but what a torrent of images, not words, I'll repeat, NOT WORDS but a torrent of images afterwards, a veritable wonderland of locking, interlocking and firmly joined images, yes, if I could only list them the way they deserve, do them justice in other words, yes, if I could only do justice, some sort of justice to these images, to memory itself, recall in sublime or even excruciating detail one, yes, just a single image as it ACTUALLY APPEARED, 'Ah,' I could then say to myself, 'so this was the way it was,' or, 'this was the way it actually appeared,' mind you, I'm not asking for much, just a single, solitary image as it actually appeared, and then, yes, please, realize, then I could move on, proceed with my dying or whatever else might be happening, I mean I just don't know, with or without clenched fists, important to note I think, in some sense I would be free then, yes, I think I just might, free of the amorphous, the suffocating grip of the past, yes, just a single transparent memory would do, free of any haze, mist, clouds, what have you, and this on some beach or THE BEACH or off, it really wouldn't matter, in other words just some memory without any HINDRANCES OR OBSTRUCTIONS, please, I'm trying to make this as simple as I possibly can, if not for your sake then mine, yes, certainly for mine, all I want, to continue with them for her, for appearance's sake.

"I didn't hear. You were looking away, Viktor."

Fear and loathing.

Or hate and love.

Nevertheless.

I manage a smile for her.

"Life, life and more life," I whisper.

Or think.

Either or.

Samantha, if that's what she's called, ah, but how lovely the way she sits, stares and pretends to listen, yes, I certainly have or had a taste in women, some at any rate, with her perfectly easy, natural way of sitting in that chair, yes, it's been weeks, I don't know how many, but weeks let's just say since I managed a similar feat, accomplishment, 'Ah, but life made up of nothing but such simple feats, accomplishments, 'I tell myself, just sitting in a chair in that fashion I mean, an absence, yes, a total absence of self-consciousness, although I'm only guessing, the very simplicity breathtaking I might add, ah, if only there were some way, any way at all of conveying this to her, yes, that might very well put our relationship on a different footing, the past as well as the present I'm talking about, ah, but in the end the bother of it all, you get my drift I think, but the bother of finding words, yes, just the RIGHT WORDS and then actually pronouncing them, both becoming increasingly difficult although the latter more than the former, MUCH MORE than the former, words as if mere obstacles now, much the way notations on a music sheet had become obstacles once, in time and with time I'm talking about, 'This' I tell myself, 'yes, this is what happens when fear enters,' or hesitation or doubt or a general or specific sense of abandon, of hopelessness, bear with me, but the fact is or the FACT REMAINS that while I might have any of number of things to say to this so-called Samantha, my last wife if I'm not mistaken, I simply can't, CAN NOT, and this puts a damper, I don't see how it wouldn't, but a damper on her so-called visit and our attempts to communicate, I, meaning she, but she might as well say, 'Ah, what big eyes you have,' or nose or lips or teeth, although my teeth, most of them at any rate, no longer my own, I add this apropos of nothing or in the way of clarification if you prefer, yes, FURTHER CLARIFICATION, but I can no longer hear, focus on what she is saying, it comes and goes as do most or perhaps even ALL THINGS, but Samantha and her words go in in and out of focus, it can't be helped, just the way things are.

"Here. Look. Look what I've brought you."

I just don't know.

But photographs, some, a few, quite a number in fact, no, I couldn't be mistaken about something like that, but, BUT, she shuffles them like cards before handing them to me, that's the impression I have, and then, yes, she hands them to me one at a time, and, "Look, look, look," she repeats, even though she can see, yes, ABSOLUTELY SEE that I have a hard enough time simply holding or holding on to them, but that doesn't seem to bother her, no, not in the least, and then, "Can you tell me who that is?" or that, in other words some other that, as though this were some kind of test or even a contest, in other words guess the identity, the RIGHT IDENTITY and I'll win a prize, god only knows what sort but neither she nor I give a damn, please, note, I DON'T GIVE A DAMN, but, "This is you," she points, "and this I," and then some, some someone else, it really makes little or no difference, I can no sooner identify myself than I can anyone else, please note, I can't identify ANYONE AT ALL, please, I'm simply looking at images of images, I hope that's clear, but IMAGES OF IMAGES when I have a hard enough time looking at the peculiar images in my head, and I'm not even speaking of identifying, no, identification an entirely different issue, but Samantha, if that's what she's called, if that's who she is, appears to be filled with confidence and hope, please, note, both HOPE AND CONFIDENCE and the last thing I want is to disappoint, I mean hasn't my life, or anyone's life for that matter, but my life let's just say, hasn't my life been filled with disappointments galore, all our lives filled with nothing but disappointments in the end, I'll go on, but, no, I want nothing more to do with disappointments, not if I can help it, so, so, "Amazing" I simply tell this so called Samantha without in any way clarifying just what I mean by this singular word, yes, she is on her own as far as that goes, and, yes, LET HER BE ON HER OWN I'm thinking, we all are in the end, she no different than I or Anne or Anna, whoever she may be, and I hand back the photographs, in a single gesture of which I'm not unjustifiably proud, but, "No, no, they're for you, for you to keep," in other words my gesture, by no means effortless, entirely wasted, I nod, no, no smile this time but I do manage a nod and drop the photographs on my blanket, my belly beneath the blanket to be more precise, and she, no, I'm not sure what she does afterwards, by then I've had enough, ENOUGH, I shut my eyes as though she were no longer there, if she ever was, and I feel myself descend, no, fall, better I think, but fall into a blank darkness, or bottomless pool, whichever you prefer.

Things go on.

The way they always have?

No, that's saying too much or too little.

Things go on let's just say and stick to that.

Yes.

Is vertigo a necessary condition, a by-product for someone near the end?

Rhetorical question.

Or not.

Let's go on.

Yes.

But.

At this point I would like to make the following statement.

My attitude exceptional.

Are you listening?

MY ATTITUDE EXCEPTIONAL.

And while I'm somewhat, note, just somewhat in the dark as to what I mean by this, it's still something of a fact, or close enough at any rate, even Ms. Boyer or Anne or Anna remarked on it, in fact, "My, but we're looking chipper this morning," she said the other day, and while 'chipper' is another one of those words open to divergent interpretations, I for one, ah, here we go, but I for one took it for a comment about my EXCEPTIONAL ATTITUDE, I was sitting on the edge of my bed, please note, not in my bed but already or finally or at last on the very edge of it, and ready, yes, as if ready for any further developments, yes, as far as standing and some sort, any sort of movement was concerned, I hadn't in days although I could have easily been mistaken, hours, days, weeks at times difficult to separate, to tell apart in my head, no matter, and in fact I subsequently did move, walk about a bit, around the room, down the corridor and perhaps, PERHAPS even out onto the grounds to catch some rays of the blessed sun, yes, but that may be going a bit too far, in fact I'm almost sure it is, no matter, let's just say I DID MOVE with Ms. Boyer's willing and able assistance, or unwilling but still moderately able assistance, my arm in hers or hers in mine, and no doubt we made, although I have my doubts, but perhaps we made what people sometimes refer to as A HANDSOME COUPLE, oh, but how I make myself smile, even laugh at times, I actually do, at any rate off, off we went, where and for how long of no great importance, in other words I couldn't and still can't say, no matter, but all that fodder for the imagination, later on I mean, yes, one can only hope, but then, yes, EVEN THEN there seemed to be a new if not entirely brand new opening for and between the two of us, please, I just hope you're following, at any rate it was something, I'm just saying, but something of a momentous occasion, it may well have been, and perhaps, yes, PERHAPS she even started telling me some sections, selections or certain highlights of the story of her life, no, not the entire story of course, that would have hardly been possible, and I the same, in other words some sections, selections and certain highlights of my life, although I rather doubt it because of my faulty, my erratic memory, and even with a so-called EXCELLENT MEMORY I doubt I would have been able to make, to choose any number of sections, selections let alone the so-called highlights of my life, nevertheless the fact remains, what fact, ah, please, but the fact remains that Anne or Anna and I were in some sense on our way, to getting ever closer I mean, no, I don't think I could or would be mistaken about something like this, yes, let's just say I'm not, at any rate whatever happened on that particular day or morning to be precise, and all, please, listen, all because of my EXCEPTIONAL ATTITUDE, and, no, I can't, I simply can't make it any clearer than this.

How things stand then.
Is that right?
But how things stand or stood.
Yes, safer in the past I think.
Was it Beethoven or Mahler or perhaps even Mozart?
On shaky grounds for sure, it could well have been one or the other or all three perhaps with some others thrown in for good or bad measure.
Yes.
But as far as I recall it had always been Beethoven or Mahler or even Mozart perhaps, yes, let's focus on them while leaving the others aside for the moment, simpler for us both I think, and SIMPLICITY THE KEY, yes, I'm becoming more and more convinced of this if I'm not already, ENTIRELY I mean, but first Mozart then Beethoven then Mahler, although the order not at all important, but was there ever a time, in my life, in the past

I mean when first Mozart then Beethoven then Mahler weren't important, and by important I mean essential, yes, as essential as air, food and water, have I left out anything, no, I don't think so, but throughout my entire life, the past I mean, I wanted nothing less than to emulate, to become part of that select group of musical geniuses who somehow managed to convey or at any rate grab a hold of something GRAND, something REAL, although the two not necessarily and certainly not always related, no, indeed, but I believe I saw my life, in the past I mean, as a calling, a challenge to enter that select group of musical geniuses who appeared to make an immense difference or at any rate a difference to the lives of others and to their own as well I suppose, yes, I think that goes without saying but, BUT from the start, from the very outset I think I realized that this was NOT TO BE, that no matter how hard I would try, and here I deserve some credit, yes, I think I do, but that no matter how hard I would try I would never be a part of that select group of musical geniuses who truly COUNTED, who truly MADE A DIFFERENCE, that in the beginning as well as at the end I would be nothing more than an amateurish composer of insignificant music or an insignificant composer of amateurish music, that something, yes, something would always elude or keep me from becoming a composer who TRULY MATTERED, who in a musical fashion was able to do battle with that something ESSENTIAL in life, to grasp and to convey that ALL IMPORTANT something in life, that in the beginning as well as the end I would never arouse the emotions, the feelings in listeners that a Mozart, a Beethoven or a Mahler had always aroused in me, that I would never, please, note, NEVER be able to impart that clear, that unified vision that only music of the highest quality is capable of imparting, and this no matter how hard I would try, or wouldn't, that I would be doomed to forever wallow in the shallows without ever venturing into the depths, the DEEP WATERS that truly mattered, that in choosing to be a so-called composer, a man of music I was simply choosing to be an impostor, a fake, that only by becoming a fake, an impostor would I ever be able to refer to myself as a so-called composer, a man of music, that short of simply and ENTIRELY turning my back on music I was doomed to live my life as an impostor, a fake, but this I could never do, no, I simply COULD NOT.

Yes.

And this was how things stood and or continue to stand
In a manner of speaking.

And now, yes, of course, now I simply find it impossible to listen to Mozart or Beethoven or even Mahler, the noises all about, from the street for example, much more appealing, comforting to me, and as for my own music, no, I have absolutely no wish to think about let alone discuss it, and while I occasionally do think about a Mozart or a Beethoven or a Mahler, never, not for a single moment do I ever think about myself as a composer in the past, I run from it as if from a plague, from damnation itself as it were.

'Simplify, Viktor, simplify.'
Sound advice.
The best I think.
Or.
'Look, Viktor, simply look. And see.'
The same. Very nearly.
The bed, the window, the table, the chair.
I could go on.
The ceiling, the walls, the floor, the door.
Let me repeat, the DOOR.
And everything within and without, in other words what's kept in and what out, simple enough I think, objects seen and others merely imagined, 'oh, but there's a world out there, Viktor,' or even an ENTIRE WORLD out there, it makes one think of course, I don't see how it wouldn't, and leading, I'm just hypothesizing, but leading to a certain CLARITY OF VISION, I'm just saying, and easy, please, follow, how easy it would be if this were actually the case, and amazing, yes, even AMAZING perhaps, but once again I'm only saying, but, BUT what if the world were just one certain, singular and specific way and no other, in other words everything seen and or imagined just one way and no other, in other words a chair just a chair, a table a table and a window a window, please, this is not just a game I'm playing but getting at something, yes, DEFINITELY something, although you needn't take my word for it, not at all, just follow along is all I'm asking, but what if, WHAT IF one could subtract all hesitation, doubt

and uncertainty from one's vision, in other words WHAT IF what one saw was exactly what one saw and nothing, please, absolutely NOTHING ELSE, a heady concept you must admit, and the same for people of course, in other words people exactly the same as one saw them, who and what they were exactly the same as they appeared, one's expectations fully met and in no way tested, trifled with, that would be something, I think you'll agree, but some SOMETHING for sure, a total or near total absence of confusion, of doubt.

I wet my bed.

Here we go.

With all this thinking, theorizing I wasn't paying much attention, serves me right for disregarding this simplest of urges, I mean thinking is one thing but pissing all over yourself something else, an occurrence or event, if you will, both quantitatively as well as qualitatively different, talk about setting yourself up to fail, although even with ATTENTION soiling oneself often unpreventable, but let's be clear, yes, PERFECTLY CLEAR for just once, I'm here to wet, to soil myself and others, Anne or Anna for example, but others, any number of others here to clean, to cleanse me, ah, but what a lovely word, 'cleanse, ' I just hope you appreciate, but here I and there the others, any and all others, and the relationship between us, if one may call it such, that between cleanser and cleansed, yes, and this may well be the beginning as well as the end, although I strongly suspect the latter, please, note, THE END, and even though I have no idea, or just a few, about what this has to do with simplifications, it still might, you see, IT STILL MIGHT, I mean is there any simpler and or more essential relationship than that between cleanser and cleansed, yes, I would even suggest that some are born to be cleansed and others to cleanse, with some, occasional changing of roles of course, depending on time, place and various other CIRCUMSTANCES, in other words as we move, shift, shuffle and muddle through life our roles never clearly, absolutely defined, once and for all I mean, the cleansers frequently becoming the cleansed and the other way around, there is really no telling, guessing in advance, in other words we simply deal with our roles, our frequently or even constantly shifting roles when and as they come up, yes, I don't see where we have much or even any choice in the matter, but now, right now I'm talking about, it's fairly obvious that I'm the cleansed and she, WHOEVER, the cleanser, and I only wish there were some way of changing, turning this around, yes, even for a short, the briefest period of time, I would be satisfied I think, return from being the cleanser to the cleansed once more with few if any complaints, BUT this is not to be, I just hope you realize, this is no longer TO BE.

Ah.
But how she walked into my life.
Who, when where?
Immaterial.
I prefer her nameless of course, but given my condition this may be of necessity rather than preference, but nameless, let's just say, I increasingly find names not at all essential for images, yes, certain images in my head, we'll move on, yes, and it was her movements, her walk that first caught my eye, my attention, walking towards me as I recall, yes, along some nowhere path in the middle of some nowhere park unless I'm very much mistaken, and looking neither left, right, up, down but straight, yes, strictly straight ahead, in other words not looking at me as she approached, no, not at all, although I was looking at her from the moment I noticed her, from the VERY START that is, but she, yes, she only looked at me when it became unavoidable, when I shifted my walk, my direction, if ever so slightly, to block her path, ah, but the nerve, the guts, the air of self-confidence I had in those days, or the DRIVE, the PASSION for things all about me, which in this instance included her, yes, her first and foremost, and she stopped, yes, no, I just hope you realize that even though it had been I to have blocked her, she would not have walked into my life unless she herself had stopped as well, in other words at that moment everything depended not only my initial action but her equal and opposite reaction as it were, and then, yes, in time and with time she most definitely WALKED INTO MY LIFE, although I'm no longer sure what I mean by this, everything and nothing I suppose, but I can safely assert, although can one ever, no matter, but I can assert, let's just say, that for some time afterwards we were as if inseparable, as ONE I'm tempted to say although that may be going a bit too far, but for some time afterwards it was she and I and I and she, a most comfortable if not entirely perfect fit, and this went on and on and on until, what,

something, some something or some other something happened, hard to know at this distance in time, but was it or was it not grand while it lasted, the only question I think, WAS IT OR WAS IT NOT GRAND WHILE IT LASTED, yes, the only question worth asking in the long run as well as the short.

Yes.

I'm fairly sure.

Who, when, where?

Ah, but how serious one gets about these things, how one, or at least a part of one simply refuses to LET GO.

Doing one's utmost to cling, to hang on might be another way of putting it.

Or finding a handle, that ALL IMPORTANT HANDLE to everything in the past as well as the present.

Which doesn't exist.

Of course not.

Oh, but how I make myself smile, even laugh out loud at times. 'Viktor,' I even tell myself, 'Viktor, you're okay so long as you can still entertain yourself from time to time.' Note the pronoun.

Important I think.

But we'll go on.

What else, really, WHAT ELSE for now?

Yes. No. Maybe.

In the past as well as the present and any POSSIBLE FUTURE, you see how I'm still thinking, planning ahead, something, something, SOMETHING will come to me, it always has, and then, yes, I'll be once more who I once was or still am or will possibly become, although such a thing not easy to contemplate, in fact well nigh impossible, but here is what I think, no, I have no more patience for thoughts, the thinker and his thoughts, are they or are they not one and the same after all, in other words if no thoughts then no thinker, yes, that's about the size of it, and fearless, yes, one must be absolutely fearless in facing this reductive but completely essential fact, IF NO THOUGHTS THEN NO THINKER, I just hope you see the horrendously beautiful or beautifully horrendous implications of this, THE THINKER SIMPLY DOES NOT EXIST, and I only wish I could push this a bit further, where, I'm not sure, but just a bit further than this, but I'm no longer capable if I ever was, that's the thing, I'M NO LONGER CAPABLE.

Ah, but how time passes.

No matter what, I mean.

And in and through time, please follow, this tremendous longing still, please, note the adjective, carefully chosen I assure you, but this longing which is all, yes, at times ALL THERE IS, although for what, terrific question, FOR WHAT, you'll excuse me if I won't answer, won't even try, yes, no, maybe is about the best I can come up with, which is really no answer, no, not even close, but at this stage of my waning existence am I or am I not allowed questions without answers, yes, I'll leave that for you to decide, but simple and or complicated answers no longer sufficient, in other words they just DON'T SUFFICE if they ever have.

Ah, the minutes.

Or the hours, the days, the weeks and so on and so forth.

But there must be another, a different way of regarding time, other than quantitatively I mean, in other words this happened then this then this, or even the reverse, neither this happened nor that nor something else, eventually one grows SICK AND TIRED of nothing but measurements and comparisons, of regarding, looking at time through time itself, there must be another, a different way, looking at time from without and not within.

Don't mind me.

I'm simply thinking, speculating.

It's a lovely day.

Early or late morning, afternoon, whatever.

Yes, better I think.

And when was the last time, the ABSOLUTE LAST when I thought or said this to myself, one minute, hour, day pretty much the same as the last, traps, yes, nothing but traps as far as I am concerned, but now, A LOVELY DAY I just thought or said to myself, a palpable difference, please note, acknowledge.

The open window.

Can I continue?

And the birds if there are any birds, the flowering trees, I could go on but you get my point I think, and it isn't necessary, not at all ABSOLUTELY ESSENTIAL that I actually see them, no, hearing and smelling sufficient for the time being, in other words the sounds as well as the scents, yes, at times like these I come very close to SURPRISING MYSELF, 'Still alive, Viktor,' I even comment to myself, in other words someone who can still hear and smell is still among the living, by definition as it were.

But, 'It's a lovely day,' let's just say and let it go at that.

And the light.

Of course.

A lovely quality as well as angle, and just now, why not, but just now I am reminded of Goethe' s dying words, "Light, light and more light," and even if he was exaggerating, no, I wouldn't put it past him, still I see what he was after, what he may have meant, although, please, note, ALTHOUGH if he hadn't been Goethe he could as easily have said, 'Dark, dark and more dark, ' six of one and half dozen of the other as far as I'm concerned.

But it's a lovely day.

Ah, but how I wish it were simpler, yes, just a bit simpler than this, in other words simpler than the light, the birds, the flowering trees, but, no, perhaps this is simple enough, as simple as it can possibly get.

Yes.

And then the following.

Please mark.

'I won't survive this spring.'

In other words this my last, my final and therefore eternal spring, a bit of a jump, I know, but I don't see myself surviving into summer and beyond, so this is my eternal spring, and finally, I don't know, but finally I may just be looking at time from without and not within, although that's questionable, nothing but wishful thinking in the end.

I'll go on.

Ms. Boyer enters.

Or Anne or Anna.

Or the great UNKNOWN.

Which is how I often think of her.

All others as well in fact, women, men, children, it hardly matters, all of them the GREAT UNKNOWNS as far as I'm concerned, and I to them of course, it stands to reason, I'll let you in on a little secret in life, my own little secret, NO ONE EVER GETS TO KNOW ANYONE ELSE, in other words all of us great unknowns as far as the rest of us are concerned, what need for a so-called god then as the GREAT UNKNOWN when we have millions, billions of lesser but equally GREAT UNKNOWNS surrounding us every moment, every day of our lives, I'm simply saying, suggesting, feel free to think it out for yourself, far be it from me to impose any sort of approach in this regard.

Ah, but the birds, the scents, the light.

Or Anne or Anna enters, which is where we were, the very last thing I believe.

My eyes still sensitive to her appearance, my ears to her steps, my nose, but you get my drift I think, STILL SENSITIVE is what I'm trying to convey, in fact assert, and "How goes it with you?" I even ask, I who almost never initiate any sort of conversation, any kind of give and take, only hope I took her by surprise, trust me, not easy, no, certainly not with a woman like that, surprise almost always on her side and never, hardly ever on mine, but the last thing I want just now is to impart the appearance of a man on his last legs, which I am of course, no question, but appearance half the battle as far as I'm concerned, let me elaborate, I may be gurgling, sighing, squeaking, groaning, the works, but what, really, WHAT do all those matter so long as I'm still capable of putting on a courageous front, she approaches, steps close, looks down, here we go, and then, THEN our eyes meet, oh, how I've been longing to be able to say such a sentence, for days, weeks, perhaps even months now, hard to say, but, 'Then their eyes met,' read such a sentence in some cheap romance novel and you know exactly what is happening with a fairly good guess of what is to follow, and while I'm not predicting that here, right here and now anything is about to follow, still, it's lovely to be able to say, "Then their eyes met," and leave the rest to chance, to fate, in other words our extremely limited and limiting circumstances.

Windows to the soul.

Why not?

One can always speculate, hope.

And I don't know how long we hold the gaze, our gazes, useless to theorize without sufficient evidence for certainty, but the time lapsed or elapsed emboldens a further question from me, yes, one more, "Could it be you and me, Anna?" please note the clarity, the very strength of such a question, no, I no longer thought I was capable, but here I and there she, or there I and here she, and while I can well imagine more propitious circumstances as well as more suitable lovers, potential of course, still, a question like that, it certainly cuts to the chase, the very heart of the matter, at the very least it calls for a more than ordinary, run-of-the-mill response, in other words what else is a question like that but a blatant refusal to accept THINGS AS THEY ARE, to accede to the STATUS QUO, I think you'll agree, and her response, while not openly encouraging, isn't entirely, COMPLETELY discouraging, "What's gotten into you, Viktor?" note the use of the name, Viktor, a first I think although I could be mistaken, but mistaken about something like this, no, I don't think so, in fact I'm quite sure.

Shall I repeat her response, her own question?

Perhaps it isn't necessary.

All the same, "What's gotten into you, Viktor?"

And the rest as they say is history or will be or just might

I mean one never knows.

"What's gotten into you, Viktor?"

I just hope you see.

One morning or afternoon or evening or night.

Difficult to pin down of course, I won't even try, but dreaming, that much for certain, I was or must have been dreaming at the time.

But in the dream, whenever it was, the music of Beethoven with the force of an explosion in my head, in other words the music of Beethoven exploding in my head, Beethoven whose music may have been the most explosive ever written, and Beethoven himself, who may have been the most explosive individual, composer who ever walked this miserable earth, I'm just saying, but Beethoven the man who was always on the verge or actually exploding throughout his entire life, and his music of course, the music of a true genius that fully, entirely, COMPLETELY mirrored the nature, the soul, the VERY ESSENCE of that explosive man, and was there anything, I mean ANYTHING AT ALL I wanted someone to think or say about me except this, yes, that here, here was an EXPLOSIVE MAN, an EXPLOSIVE CREATOR, in other words someone who completely found as well as lost himself in his music, who effectively became HIS MUSIC and in the process the ENTIRE WORLD ITSELF, no matter, and it was the Fifth, of course, Beethoven's Fifth Symphony that exploded in my head, what else, and even though that piece of music, especially its VERY START has become a cliché of sorts by now, no, that didn't stop it from exploding in my head, all great works of art, pieces of music in danger of becoming clichés after the fact, in and with the passage of time of course and to the ordinary, the common viewer or listener of course, but no, NOT TO ME, not when it EXPLODED IN MY HEAD, please appreciate, the very start, the first four notes especially, as fresh, as bright, as CLEAR as at the moment they had been birthed in Beethoven' s head, in fact, nothing, please note, NOTHING LESS than a call to arms, to action, and while throughout my life I could fully hear and completely appreciate this, I could never, no, NEVER EVEN APPROACH creating something of the same immediacy, the same power, these four simple notes I'm talking about, and then push on, rush along from there of course, in other words something, that ESSENTIAL SOMETHING always lacking in me, that spark, that fire, that undeniable touch of genius, and because of this, in other words in time and with time what else could I do but distance myself from the music of Beethoven, from all music in fact especially my own, but none of this mattered in the dream, yes, when I finally heard the music of Beethoven explode in my head, although now I'm simply recollecting, telling and dreams notorious for recollecting, for telling, perhaps even more notorious for recollecting, for telling than anything REAL that actually happened to one, nevertheless it may well be worth the effort, I'm not sure, but it just might.

Ah, the light of my life.
How do I know?
No matter, I just do.

But Lucia the light of my life, although the name made up, I'm almost certain, the coincidence too great, but Lucia let's just say who one day appeared as if out of nowhere, as most, perhaps even all the pivotal persons in my life appeared out of nowhere, more or less I'm talking about, and, yes, she was quite unlike anyone else I had ever met before, up to that point at any rate, and was or was it not love at first sight, let me repeat, was or was it not LOVE AT FIRST SIGHT, such things do happen, let me assure you, first nothing and then something, yes, something of even TREMENDOUS IMPORTANCE, and, 'Whoever loved who loved not at first sight?' yes, this line, not my own, seems to echo in my head from time to time, but, no, it wasn't Lucia at all, it was Lucy as I recall, although the difference so slight as to be negligible, so, Lucy, please remember, and although I'm necessarily short on descriptive details, let me just say the following, she, Lucy turned night into day and day into night as far as I was concerned, in other words a regular Lucifer before the fall, before she became Satan, although, yes, here we go, ALTHOUGH she had one good leg and one bad if I'm not mistaken, or one leg somewhat, just a bit shorter than the other, which gave a peculiar although entirely endearing lilt or tilt or, to put it more simply, slant to her walk, ah, but how clearly I can see it, feel it, even taste it, now, right now I mean, and far from being an obstacle to my unstoppable, in fact overwhelming passion for her it became its very SOURCE, in fact its ESSENCE, yes, as did her lazy eye, the left if I'm not mistaken, the left that looked left when the other, the right looked straight ahead, other variations as well of course which I no longer have the head to work out, no matter, and as for breasts, the one large, the other small, although just which was which I can no longer clearly recall, but sufficient I think, yes, to remark on the noticeable difference between the two, and a lisp, ah, here we go, but a lisp or even a slight stutter or at the very least a certain difficulty with the pronunciation of certain letters or even entire words, quite lovable I assure you, but, oh, how she made the sun rise and the moon, or the moon set and the sun, six of one as far as I'm concerned, and all our sighs, whispers with the not infrequent exclamations, WORDS in other words and CRIES of which I'm no longer capable, it makes me sweat and shudder, shudder and sweat to think of it, now I mean, although the cause for those may well be something unrelated, in other words ENTIRELY DIFFERENT, not important, but was there, will there ever be another Lucia or Lucy, ah, that is the question, but I have still a better or at any rate more relevant one, if she walked through that door right now would I still love her the way I once did, or, here we go, would I even RECOGNIZE HER or she me, a mind, a brain splitting headache all I'm certain of at the moment, yes, that in addition to my shivers, my sweat, memory the cause, Lucia or Lucy the cause, or something, here we go, something or someone ALTOGETHER DIFFERENT, but once more, once again or STILL this ABSOLUTE NEED to get to the bottom of things, of a single thing at any rate, was or was it not Lucia or Lucy, you understand the question I trust, and was or was she not the LIGHT OF MY LIFE, here, I think I've got it, she had a missing finger, the left hand, I'm quite certain, the index or the pinky, yes, things a bit hazy here, but the thing, the MAIN THING was that MISSING FINGER, which made me love her above any and all other women, made her in fact the LIGHT OF MY LIFE, this is all I'm saying, trying to get across, as for the rest I no longer give a damn, yes, let's get this clear, the rest as if with nothing, ABSOLUTELY NOTHING to do with me.

Yes.

But why do I still care, continue, push on in this pretend, make-believe fashion, anyone else, please note, ANYONE ELSE in my unenviable state would have called it quits a long time ago, in other words why prolong the inevitable, the pain, the uncertainty, the frustration of my CONTINUED EXISTENCE, my so-called life no longer a life, per se I mean, the legs as good as gone, the arms, the shoulders and, yes, even THE HEAD, although different parts to different degrees depending on the day, the hour or even the minute, in other words nothing straightforward, nothing with any predictability one can rely on, days and or hours or even minutes when I start from a supine or sitting or even, god help me, standing position, or continue I suppose, and 'Now, Viktor, now you'll succeed at last,' I even tell myself, please note the irony, the sheer mockery of such a thought, hardly worth going into, but it's in such a position, in other words supine or sitting or even standing, that Anne or Anna will find, come upon me, in other words continue to intrude upon my life as I no doubt continue to intrude upon hers, and, "Still taking it easy, Viktor?" she'll remark, or,

"Already up, Viktor?" or, simply, "Look at you, Viktor!" her words of little or no consequence as far as I'm concerned, or of some, yes, let's be fair, occasionally of some to be sure, and then we go through our routines which appear to vary while stubbornly REMAINING THE SAME, the examinations, the pills, the tubes, the injections, feel free to take your pick, and then, yes, what follows is anybody's guess, although the other morning or afternoon or evening she, that is Anne or Anna simply sat as I lay or sat or even stood, I'm not sure which, and started talking, articulating, in other words holding forth about some things, a number of things in her life, of some importance to be sure , I have no doubt, in other words any number of things she must have felt she had to get off her chest, right then and there I mean, and while I did my best or what amounted to my best to listen, in my then unsatisfactory state or condition or what you will I found it difficult if not impossible to listen as well as hear, please note, to LISTEN AS WELL AS HEAR, a hard time then to understand not only the gist of what she was saying but the order in which she was saying it, I only wished she could have, would have picked another time and place or another time at any rate because the place is always or nearly always the same, but another time when I was feeling a bit more like myself, which is a laugh of course as by now I lack any clear idea of what that MYSELF entails or once entailed, no matter, but the fact remains that at that particular time and place all she wanted was to talk and I for my part to listen, I only hope that's clear, but, no, it wasn't possible, the talking, yes, but not the LISTENING AND HEARING at the same time, nods, yes, just a few nods were all I could manage, and it's a shame, it really is or was, for who knows when she'll be in the mood to UNBURDEN, to REVEAL herself in such a fashion again, because while being unable to both LISTEN AND HEAR I still had the feeling that in talking, holding forth Anne or Anna was both UNBURDENING as well as REVEALING herself, and later, somewhat or much later I would think to myself what an opportunity missed or squandered, and how likely the chances that such an occasion or opportunity would come again, and for the longest time afterwards I tried to resurrect, to replay her words in my mind, along with the accompanying feelings of course, but all my subsequent attempts, efforts in vain, I only succeeded in increasing my splitting headache with its accompanying nausea, please note, headache and nausea both, and after a while I had no choice but to SURRENDER, in other words give up on trying to recall, to resurrect Anne or Anna's words along with their accompanying emotions, ALTHOUGH then, yes, I would have gladly settled for just the emotions without the words, they would have sufficed I think, but no, and, 'Here we go, Viktor, here we go,' I said to myself on the loss of yet another significant, although how can one be sure, but let's just say another SIGNIFICANT moment in my life, but let me be clear, THE DISEASE TOOK OVER, as it often, frequently or nearly always does, in time and with time I mean, and once again it became perfectly clear that I belonged to this disease and not the other way around, or that at any rate by now this DISEASE AND I were as good as inseparable, in other words the same, EXACTLY THE SAME ENTITY, and no matter how hard I tried or would try to insert something or someone to separate the two it was bound to end in failure, and then luckily, or not, I fell into a dreamless, bottomless sleep, although on waking I seemed to recall lugworms all around, dark against the darkness of my dreamless sleep, but to call that sleep, no, I wouldn't validate it with such a label, but the main thing was this sense of loss, that Anne or Anna was lost to me then, along with others, yes, so many others of the past but of the present as well.

Not easy.
May I go on?
Now and again I get visions, although glimpses more accurate, yes, just GLIMPSES of myself sitting down at a piano, but not just any piano, no, MY PIANO with and in its familiar surroundings, the details unimportant, but MY PIANO near MY WINDOW in the past, if memory serves I always depended on natural light for my so called composing, the evenings, the nights taken up with other activities, let's let those go, but I was always a so-called daytime composer which showed, of course it showed in the light, the ephemeral nature of my compositions, I never or HARDLY EVER composed from so-called waves or even seizures of inspiration, in fact I mistrusted them the way one mistrusts the various angels and or demons of one's imagination, all those magnificent and or horrible creatures that reside only in the dark, in the night, in the dark,

in the night I was otherwise occupied as already mentioned, but I had this mistaken perhaps even destructive notion that I could become or even be a so-called serious composer without tackling my angels, my demons head on, in the dark, in the night that is, and this aside from the occasionally painful but nearly always OBVIOUS realization that while blessed with a modest amount of talent I lacked the genius, the ABSOLUTE GENIUS of a Mozart, a. Beethoven or even a Mahler, in other words composers of the first rank who did not shy away from taking on their angels and demons, who in tackling their angels and demons also and MOST ESPECIALLY tackled themselves, no, this, yes, both as a so-called composer as well as a man this was the last, the VERY LAST thing on my mind, and this, yes, all this was reflected in my music, that here, yes, here was a composer, a man who persistently shied away from or simply refused to TACKLE HIMSELF, who simply sat down at his daytime piano as if arriving at some unimportant, insignificant job, a job just as adequately performed by thousands if not millions of others, and the curious, the frightening thing, in retrospect of course, was that for years I succeeded in this false, this fake approach to music, to LIFE ITSELF perhaps, in other words for years I succeeded in fooling others along with myself, and rather than consider me an INTERESTING COMPOSER, all the critics, the audiences would have been much better off if they had recognized me for the FAKE, the IMPOSTOR I truly was, and this from the start, the very outset perhaps, and I, yes, of course, I myself would have been much better off to have seen this clearly myself, because then, you see, yes, then I might just have found the resolution, the courage, the abandon to start tackling myself, and, yes, even if the results, musical and otherwise, would have been mediocre and perhaps even destructive, it would have been better to have destroyed myself instead of waiting for life to accomplish it piecemeal, yes, all at once or not at all as with a Mozart, a Beethoven or even a Mahler, but, see, yes, just see how I exhaust myself, run circles around the past in the present, it's no good I tell you, absolutely no good at all.

Another vision, another glimpse.

I sit down at my daytime piano, but then instead of touching the keys, or playing around with certain facile sounds, I start pounding with my fists, and not just the keys but the entire piano until it's smashed to a hundred, a thousand, a million pieces, and then, please follow, with my bloodied fingers I sit down at my nighttime piano, later on that is, and it is on this, this nighttime piano that I truly begin to compose, and for the very first time I lose myself in the challenge, the work, the struggle, and in the end nothing, but NOTHING is left of me but my music, which may or may not survive, it goes without saying, but the main thing is that the music, ONLY THE MUSIC would be left.

Do I go on?

Visions, even glimpses with a certain annoying, exhausting quality.

I think you'll agree.

But.

DO I GO ON?

Life without her not worth living. Yes, but who?

Yes, that's the question all right.

But nameless, yes, yet another nameless one, amazing how the mind censors, escapes into forgetting, some things of course while leaving others fully intact, but NAMELESS let's just say while any and all emotions aroused by HER as keen as when they were first felt, and when I say life without her was not worth living it's her I have in mind, no one but HER.

Worth pursuing?

Yes, if only to counteract, to balance the pain in my throat and chest.

SHE.

Here we go.

And the simple or complicated truth of the matter, no, simple, let's just say simple, the simple truth of the matter was that she rejected me, yes, first enticed then rejected me, and the very reason for my great and enduring, although who's to say, but my great love for her was her rejection of me, first the enticement then the rejection, in other words the very reason for my thinking, saying that LIFE WITHOUT HER WAS NOT WORTH LIVING, which still holds to a certain degree, was her ultimate, definitive rejection of me, and once again, ah, here we go, SHE was no stereotypical beauty or beautiful stereotype, ankles too thick, hands too broad and face with some, I'm not sure which, but just certain masculine features, yes, the eyebrows and the very slant of the lips perhaps, but at one time, and what a time it was, I wanted nothing more than to cling to those thick ankles, hold those broad hands and kiss those misshapen lips, yes, I think I would have willingly sacrificed, traded every single moment of the rest of my life to have been able to do so, but throughout our so-called relationship she steadfastly maintained her distance while holding out some hope, yes, a definite hope for its diminishing and eventual disappearance, yes, in retrospect I can safely say that I was a man as if beguiled, enchanted and ENTIRELY POSSESSED, please note, ENTIRELY POSSESSED, I could neither think straight nor eat, drink nor maintain something resembling a proper balance, my very gestures as if no longer my own, and all this because SHE was extremely skilled, either cursed or blessed at playing this elaborate but highly destructive game with me, and with others as well I can only guess, but from our very first meeting, which escapes memory by now, no matter, but from our first meeting she fashioned herself into the UNATTAINBALE ONE, and there is nothing more attractive, magnetic yet ultimately destructive than coming face to face with the UNATTAINABLE ONE, in her apartment she undressed for me while warning me not to approach, to maintain my distance, her smile, yes, at once insinuating and mocking nearly drove me crazy, ah, but she picked her victims most carefully, yes, I'm quite sure, only self-assured, confident and even highly arrogant men, in other words men FULLY EMBOLDENED by their past successes with women, and these she then proceeded to turn inside out, in fact to turn love inside out, and after her ridiculous and degrading victory she let me know in no uncertain terms that she had had enough, that it was time for me to move on and for her to DISAPPEAR ENTIRELY from life, and it was then I thought or said to myself that LIFE WITHOUT HER WAS NOT WORTH LIVING, and I just hope you appreciate the comical as well as painfully serious nature of my situation, but, and this may or may not come as a surprise to you, but it was then I wrote what I can only term my best pieces of music, and then, yes, also then that I was labeled a BELATED ROMANTIC COMPOSER, which was not only blatantly but offensively false of course, the sad, the ridiculous truth of the matter was that throughout my so-called career I was never ANY TYPE OF A COMPOSER but only a sort of meddling, an inadequate composer, but right now I mean to recollect, to discuss only HER and not at all my so-called music, I hope that's clear, THE ONE WITHOUT WHOM LIFE WAS NOT WORTH LIVING, and in some ways it still isn't, yes, let me assert, it STILL IS NOT.

Ah, but how the mind meanders, wanders, taking one now in one direction, now another, and to what purpose, my question entirely serious, TO WHAT PURPOSE, but you needn't try to answer that, questions like that without any simple or even complicated answers, questions like that best raised and then simply and entirely FORGOTTEN.

Ah, but how the mind wanders after all.

And wonders.

Simply amazing.

I blindfolded her.

Do you understand?

But, please, please listen.

I blindfolded her.

Whom?

Does it matter?

Why?

But BLINDFOLDED her because I meant to, set out to turn her into everyone and no one, yes, because all my life, throughout my entire life I desired everyone and no one, tell me you understand, in other words a woman who was ALL WOMEN or a love that was ALL LOVE if you will, in other words the general in the specific which is impossible of course, and while fully aware, while completely knowing this I still had to try, give it a shot, I started with the specific then, how else, but then by disguising, by hiding the specific I fully intended to move on, to POSSESS the GENERAL or UNIVERSAL if that makes it any or somewhat clearer to you, but let's just say that it was important that I'd be the only one to see and she the one to be seen, but there's no easy or simple way to explain this, let me just say that I had no intention of being reflected, caught in her eyes while I fully intended to reflect, to catch her in mine, not possible of course, you don't have to tell me, but while negating her existence for herself I simply meant to reinforce and magnify mine, you see where this is heading I'm sure, but I the single, solitary male or LOVER and she the GENERAL or the UNIVERSAL FEMALE or BELOVED, in other words the object, that's correct, the OBJECT of all my longings, my desires, and then in possessing her I would possess it ALL, but then, "Is this what you want?" she asked while I was already blindfolding her, and, "Yes, yes," I quickly replied, but too late, yes, already too late, because by asking that single, that specific question she was asserting her own single and specific existence, in other words the very thing I was after already compromised if not entirely ruined, and later, not much but somewhat later, "Ah, that's nice, yes, down there is nice," she whispered, and once again she cast a shadow over the entire ENTERPRISE, if I may call it that, once again she asserted her own separate and physical existence, and after that everything turned or returned to the specific once more, and this in spite of the fact that she was still blindfolded and I, yes, I still the only one to see without being seen, and I was already inside her when I had no choice but to tear the blindfolds from her eyes, please, appreciate, because I realized, gradually or suddenly, no matter, but I realized that there never was nor ever could be a GENERAL, a UNIVERSAL ACT OF LOVE but only numerous small, specific and therefore never ENTIRELY SATISFYING ACTS OF LOVE, and, "Why did you do that?" she asked, and this at or near the height of our mutual passion, but of course I had no reply, the joint movements of our bodies the only reply by then.

And later that afternoon or evening or night, I'm not sure which, she was all set to turn the tables, to blindfold me the way she had been blindfolded herself, and of course I had to agree, I couldn't very well refuse, but by then it was too late, the ATTEMPT or EXPERIMENT, if that's what it was a complete failure by then, but I let her try just the same, allowed her to discover this for herself.

Let's see.
A conversation, an exchange of sorts.
With Ms. Boyer, with Anne or Anna of course.
Initiated by me I might add and given verbatim or very nearly so.
And this after all the tedious and entirely useless routines of her job out of the way.

"How's my liver?"

"Enlarged."

"My kidneys?"

"Barely functioning."

"My lungs?" "

Miserable."

"My throat?"

"Shot to hell."

Straightforward, matter of fact and even staccato, yes, as a one-time musician I certainly appreciated, nothing like staccato to get one's point across, to separate fact from fiction, and Ms. Boyer or Anne or Anna extremely skilled, perhaps even gifted at separating fact from fiction, and, and here I'm merely guessing, but perhaps during her entire life, in other words not just now with miserably helpless or helplessly miserable patients like myself but for her ENTIRE LIFE, in other words judging by the present and strictly, solely by the present I see Ms. Boyer or Anne or Anna as someone wholly incapable of something as nonsensical, as ridiculous as FALLING IN LOVE for example, and this has nothing, no, ABSOLUTELY NOTHING to do with her looks which are admittedly a bit on the austere side, no, nor the way she does or doesn't do her hair and refuses any and all makeup, no, it has everything to do with her attitude, her no-nonsense, vigilant, in other words her staccato approach to life, yes, if one's entire life consists of nothing but separating fact from fiction one will never commit the absolute folly, embrace the ultimate fiction of FALLING IN LOVE, and while this has nothing to do with me, although it might, but let's just say it doesn't, but while this has nothing to do with me it does make for a certain relationship between nurse and patient, desirable as well as undesirable, desirable for its honesty of course but undesirable for, well, I'm not sure just what, but all in all it has the effect of making one occasionally explore, test the waters as it were, and after our brief conversation, exchange really, I did just that, I added, I asked one more question, "And my heart?" meaning not just the physical organ but something else as well, although it doesn't do to dwell on this, and Ms. Boyer or Anne or Anna paused and then, yes, ACTUALLY SMILED, and then simply replied, "No, there is nothing wrong with your heart as far as I can tell," a tremendous statement, yes, in or out of context, please note, and while at the time I didn't know what to make of it, and still don't, I was sure that in time and with time I would analyze it to its full, its precise meaning, and that that meaning would be something, yes, some SOMETHING for sure, but at the time, no, so I merely, simply replied, "Thank you," and she, "My pleasure, " and then, here we go, once more, once again SHE SMILED, no, I cannot emphasize, repeat this enough, SHE SMILED, and it was that smile that stayed with me and not at all our conversation, our little exchange which told me nothing I didn't already suspect, in fact fully know as well as I know the sight of my gnarled hands and the sparse, the ridiculous contents of this room.

Facing an orchestra.
Have I ever?
Yes, any number of times over my so-called career, standing straight, stiff with my back to the audience, I intensely disliked having to turn around to acknowledge the applause at the beginning as well as at the end of a performance, I made those as perfunctory, as brief as I possibly could, I never took any curtain calls, no, I simply refused no matter how ENTHUSIASTIC the reception of a particular performance, in fact the more enthusiastic the reception the more firm my resolve not to appear or reappear before the audience again, facing the orchestra however another, an entirely different matter, because only the members of an orchestra, in other words so-called musicians like myself fully comprehended, understood the absolute sham, fake nature of the conductor standing in front of them, just as it was only they, these so-called musicians to fully understand, comprehend the absolute fake, sham nature of the composition, MINE, about to be played, but here's the curious, perhaps even salutary thing, being fake, sham musicians themselves they had no problem embracing an absolutely fake, a sham composer and conductor, in other words they fully recognized themselves in me just as I completely recognized myself in them, and to see the fake as the fake and the sham as the sham was a kind of truth after all, not so the audience of course who had no, yes, ABSOLUTELY NO ABILITY to tell the fake from the real and the real from the fake, who were simply there to see and be seen as well as to hear WHATEVER should be presented to them, in other words their so-called

enthusiastic reception of whatever was played had nothing, ABSOLUTELY NOTHING to do with the quality of the music played but everything, please, listen, EVERYTHING with their disposition or predisposition to greet with enthusiasm, yes, with even a sort of wild abandon everything that was played for them, in other words their very approbation based not at all on taste but on their complete inability to distinguish the real from the fake and the other way around, and this, please listen, constituted the nature, the very essence of their lives, and if I'm somewhat, just slightly exaggerating it's merely to justify, to MAKE MY POINT, which is that I wanted nothing, no, ABSOLUTELY NOTHING to do with my so-called audience except for the briefest, the most perfunctory acknowledgement of their so called existence as well as my own, but other than that, no, ABSOLUTELY NOTHING at all, because by their very failures of hearing, of vision they made me into something I NEVER WAS nor ever WOULD or COULD BECOME, which was a real, a genuine, perhaps even a so-called important composer, and for this I couldn't forgive them, no, not then and not even now, which was why I was happy to turn my back on them as if they didn't exist and wished only that they had done the same for me, turn their backs on me as though I DIDN'T EXIST, but I'm getting carried away, I only wish you would have stopped me before I got this far, but it's the fever you see, some days worse than others, my body's last great hope of burning up all impurities along with everything else of course including my very thoughts, I'm sure you understand, exhibit some patience, some forbearance at this mental profusion, this mindless vomiting.

Ah, the truth of the matter.

But can I say that with some seriousness, with some, no matter how slight, but with some degree of conviction?

No matter.

Here we go.

I am no longer what I once WAS.

Or still AM.

Or what I'll possibly BECOME.

In other words the past not the present, and even the present not what it seems, and as for the future, yes, it's anybody's guess.

Yes.

Let me try again.

All my thoughts, feelings, emotions in which I include my pains, no, no way to disregard, to leave those out, but all my thoughts, feelings, emotions, pains as if the thoughts, feelings, emotions and even pains of someone else, someone OTHER THAN ME that is or SOME OTHER ME, and this of course leads me to the all important if not completely answerable question, WAS I EVER ENTIRELY ME, bear with me if you possibly can, but was there anything in my life I wanted as much as to be this SINGULAR, this SINGLE, this ONE entity, and, yes, I think it could have, may have, perhaps even should have been possible, through MY MUSIC of course, what else, yes, much the way Mozart, Beethoven and Mahler became these SINGULAR, SINGLE and UNIFIED entities in and through THEIR MUSIC, yes, no other way than that, their lives frequently in shambles, which was and still is there for everyone to see, no, they had ABSOLUTELY NO genius for living but for MUSIC, yes, their true originality, their genius manifesting itself only in their MUSIC, in other words it was only in their music that they became truly one, singular and entirely UNIFIED beings, in other words it was and still remains impossible to separate them from their music, the essence of a Mozart, a Beethoven, a Mahler nothing else than the very essence of their music, as for the rest of their lives they were as troubled, as ridiculous as everyone else's, as anyone's who' s ever lived, in other words they hardly mattered or in some now monotonous, now destructive ways they mattered only to themselves, but here's the thing, the only thing I'm getting at, THEIR MUSIC DID AND STILL DOES MATTER, in ways that the music of countless others, myself included of course, never did nor ever will, and this is all I'm getting at, all I'm trying to make clear, nothing but nothing about any of our lives of any significance or importance if you will but what, given enough genius, we manage to create, so that in listening to the music of a Mozart or a Beethoven or a Mahler we can unequivocally assert, 'Yes, here is Mozart the composer as well as the man' or Beethoven the composer as well as the man and Mahler the same, but in listening to my music no one but no one will ever be tempted to say that about me, in other words in listening to my music no one will ever recognize the composer as well as the man as a single, a UNIFIED ENTITY, and if throughout my meaningless career some, any number of listeners have fooled themselves into just such a recognition they were not only sadly but destructively mistaken, destructive to themselves as well as to me, because the truth of the matter was and is that in my so-called music no such UNIFICATION or UNION ever occurred, and this no matter how hard I tried or didn't, in other words it simply DIDN'T MATTER, and this is all I'm trying to point out, to clarify, because to be mistaken about something as obvious as this is to be mistaken about my entire life, my very existence, which was and still remains a useless, a meaningless life and existence, although at some level I remain more than willing to entertain any and all opposing notions, in other words, as dim as it is, some faith or hope still remains that ALL THIS HAS NOT BEEN IN VAIN, although even as we speak it's fast diminishing, I just hope you see, no doubt diminishing to NOTHING in the end.

Let's move on.
Yes, but how can we after all that?
No matter.
We'll move on.
Try something else, something new or at any rate a different approach.
Survival the key.
Now as well as then?
Hard to say.
But if in the beginning as well as near the end life isn't about survival then what, although you needn't try to answer this, what is it about?
The mind hesitates, falters, then, yes, definitely stops.
Thank god.
No way it can go beyond itself.
So then what, precisely, what is left?
We'll move on.
But if not the mind, not survival then WHAT IS LEFT?
But, please, you mustn't take seriously anything I'm saying, suggesting, asking, I'm not quite or no longer in my right mind, from time to time perhaps but, no, even that's questionable, the cancer relentless in its attacks, all my organs fair targets as far as it's concerned.

Never mind.

We push on.

And to push on, to continue is after all to start anew, please note, a BRAND NEW BEGINNING, and I say this with all the wisdom, if such it is, of a dying man, in fact every continuation something of a new start, a BRAND NEW BEGINNING, in fact, bear with me, looked at a certain way life made up of nothing but countless new starts, BRAND NEW BEGINNINGS, and with every new start, beginning one cannot discount the element of hope, in fact new starts, beginnings practically synonymous with hope, although by hope I mean nothing mysterious or, god forbid, mystical, I've lived my entire life with a healthy mistrust of the mysterious, the mystical, or the mystical at any rate because mysteries do abound, no sane man or woman would deny the mystery of a single smile or of a note perfectly played and held, but as for the mystical, please, in life what else but life and nothing of the mystical, death itself mysterious of course but, no, not at all mystical, our notions of heaven, hell and everything in between nothing but products of our frightened, our feverish imaginations, in other words imaginations FULLY ANCHORED, ENTIRELY BASED on life, no, yes, this to me was and remains so obvious as to preclude any arguments on the matter, in other words, with all due respect, I simply refuse to engage in any ARGUMENTS with you on this score, let me just repeat, the MYSTERIOUS yes, but the MYSTICAL no, in other words even someone like Anne or Anna has quite a bit of the mysterious about her but, no, not at all of the mystical, and it's that mysterious, yes, no matter how we define it, that mysterious that draws me to her, even now I mean, which is something you must admit, yes, perhaps even AMAZING when you consider my miserable, helpless and hopeless condition, yes, I think you'll agree, but the mysterious all about us, even in the very walls, ceiling and awful furnishings of this room, then how much more so in an actual human being no matter how stark, how forbidding in appearance, yes, if I can only maintain my sight, my hearing, my ability to grasp for a bit longer, but Ms. Boyer or Anne or Anna my last great project if you will, the final mystery to be embraced and solved or solved and embraced, but I might be getting carried away, it's more than likely, but only somewhat, yes, grant me this at least, only a bit given my miserable and hopeless condition.

Enough.
End of sermon.
A terrific storm brewing.

Something with an 'M'.
Millie, Mona, Maria?
I don't think so. No.
Just plain Mary?
Does it matter?
But let's just say for simplicity's sake.

At any rate it was Mary and I and I and Mary, where were we, ah, but how it all comes back, recedes then returns again, although one is never sure about the way or even what happened, I mean precisely, but we were in the woods unless I'm very much mistaken and seeking shelter, yes, some sort of shelter from the storm, but just how we got there, in other words what we were doing there something of a mystery, but Mary and I and I and Mary always in the woods, forever seeking shelter in the woods, in other words we most certainly shared this love of the woods as well as of storms I suppose, and every time we ventured into the woods there was always this possibility, even strong probability that a storm would develop, descend and catch us off guard, although not off guard, no, because, as it now seems to me, we entered the woods in the hopes of some storm enveloping and seizing us, and this one time, this particular time we got everything and more than we ever bargained for, a storm to end all storms in fact, the worst in decades in that particular part of the country, in those particular woods, driving winds, rains as well as deadly strikes of lightning, yes, the two of us running for our lives as I recall, and all this without any clear-cut goal or destination in mind, by the time we reached, came upon this cabin in the middle of the woods, in the middle of nowhere in other words, we were out of breath and soaked to the bones, the gods, fate, whatever certainly with us, protecting us that day, we broke down the door, although it may well have been unlocked, no matter, and entered another time and place, in other words someone else's past, someone else's suspended, abandoned and forgotten life, and in the process, yes, it seemed we had also suspended, abandoned and forgotten our present, our immediate lives and entered something entirely different, completely new, in other words something to do neither with the past nor the present but some altogether different, some timeless time as it were, from the time we entered we became like hungry animals tearing and clawing at one another, no, I'm not exaggerating for effect or only slightly, but if we had been lovers before, which I no longer recall, it was nothing compared to what we became in that cabin, two wild creatures with a sexual hunger that negated, obliterated anything and everything else, our very identities no longer of any consequence, our identities fully destroyed, yes, our unbridled passion at once creative and destructive or destructive and creative, in other words the storm without fully matched and even surpassed by our storms within, in other words we fell on each other with an abandon at once frightening and exhilarating, our moans, groans and cries echoed the storm's thunders, in the beginning the end and in the end the beginning I'm tempted to say, in other words creation and fall, birth and death one and the same in the violent fusion of our bodies, ah, if once, only once I had been able, capable of composing music in that vein, in other words the music of a Mozart, a Beethoven or a Mahler which at their best are fabulous, astonishing fusions of the mental and the physical, at any rate after such a passionate clash nothing, please note, NOTHING of us remained, all our thoughts, words, desires exhausted, we crawled away from each other, introduced a distance to re-capture, regain our so-called sanity, after the storm had passed we made our way separately back to town through the woods, still in sight of each other but beyond any and all possibilities of communicating, of connecting by then, and perhaps, and I'm just saying, but perhaps we never saw each other again afterwards, it's the way I would like to or actually do remember it, but this was Maria or Millie or Mary to the best of my recollection, and the woods, the storm, the cabin and everything that occurred, exploded between us, although you mustn't hold me to it, it may have been someone else and the events, the explosion described occurred in a somewhat similar although entirely different fashion.

But I don't think so.

No.

Please listen.

If the memory is real enough, what need to question details, the specifics of what actually occurred?

Fragments

Please listen.

What else but fragments after the facts, our fragmented lives, never entirely sane, whole, the ULTIMATE UNIFICATION we're after, we're all one thing one time and others at others, miserable, adequate or even accomplished lovers, composers and anything else you may think of, yet what does it matter in the end, chasing after others, ourselves, dreams in fact that forever elude or escape us as soon as we seize them, you see what I mean, we're always a step or two behind, yes, several in fact, always trying to pursue, to follow, to catch up in fact, with others, with ourselves, with dreams in fact, please, just nod if you understand, but things, please, ALL THINGS escape us in the end, but if ALL THINGS escape us in the beginning as well as at the end we do our best to escape them as well, all of us born escape artists of varying gifts and skills, in other words no sooner do we get to love someone or compose an interesting, even important piece of music than we do our best to escape them, to put them all behind us, because we are never at rest, never satisfied but always on the move, always in the process of surpassing, of becoming someone other than WHAT WE ARE, granted, a difficult concept, but in our fractured, fragmented lives we are forever seeking something of a stability, a safety that simply DOES NOT EXIST, in other words facing life we simply cannot accept the fact that we will never be safe, secure, in other words fully and entirely OURSELVES, facing our so-called lives we simply refuse to see, to acknowledge its fractured, its fragmented nature, so we breathlessly run from one thing to the next and the next, mindlessly pursue one thing and the next and the next, yes, no, and in the end nothing works, death, yes, only DEATH works in the end which finally puts a stop to all our frenzied, useless running around.

Yes.

Yes, good, bad or indifferent, with DEATH we finally step out of ourselves.

Tell me you see.

Tell me I haven't been wasting my time and yours with my ridiculous mental gymnastics.

Suddenly.

Yes, let me continue in this fashion.

At times I'm convinced that everything that happens in life happens suddenly and not at all gradually the way we think or perceive, GRADUALLY just a fiction we create for ourselves to lull ourselves into a blind acceptance of the ridiculous nature of time, we fall in and out of love SUDDENLY just as we create and destroy pieces of music suddenly, in all my life as a so-called lover of women the SUDDEN, the UNEXPECTED has been the driving force, just as in all my life as a so-called creator and destroyer of music the UNEXPECTED, the SUDDEN has been the guiding force, although to explain this any clearer than I already am, no, I don't think I'm capable.

Day breaks, night falls then day breaks again and even that's SUDDEN, take my word for it, any and all appearances to the contrary, any and all appearances not withstanding.

As a single example, take my occasional, useless, my secondhand erections.

And how's that for a topic worthy of consideration?

I just hope you have enough sympathy to bear with me for a while.

SUDDEN, my erections.

In other words as if out of nowhere, or rise, rose, risen if you prefer, in other words the sudden nature of my erections both time and place denying, believe me, something to behold as well as to hold, although given my miserable condition I abstain for the most part, yes, what else but abstain, but my SUDDEN, my UNEXPECTED erections my very last weapon against the destructive nature of TIME as well as NOTHINGNESS itself, I'm theorizing of course, but it's my sudden, my unexpected erections that in some ways still define who and what I am, in other words link me to my past as well as any possible future, I am surprised that in my so-called musical life I have never attempted to compose a symphony or even just a fugue for erections, too late now of course, but you take someone like Beethoven, what were all his serious compositions except odes to and celebrations of ERECTIONS, and Mozart the same of course except with a lighter, a more delightful touch, yes, it isn't until Wagner and Mahler that you get the mind-bending combination of ERECTIONS and DEATH, but let's not consider that for the moment, but, 'Nasty, dirty old man,' I can just hear Ms. Boyer or Anne or Anna remark, although I have never exhibited myself to her, not yet at any rate, but she couldn't, wouldn't be farther from the truth, trust me, in other words in some ways my ERECTIONS as if nothing to do with me. They're only and simply life's responses to life, in other words death defying and denying, the very 'Ding an sich' as German philosophers were fond of asserting, the things in themselves, or 'En soi, pour soi,' if you want to consider the French, in other words in and for themselves, a certain glorious assertion of life without boundaries, although a bit of a stretch to be sure, although at times I can barely hide, cover it up, hold it down in other words, in fact, 'Not yet, Viktor, not yet,' I often tell myself, yes, waiting, perhaps just waiting for the right time to unveil, to reveal, a last ditch effort for sure, but still, please listen, STILL the possibility that I will yet mount or be mounted, and then, yes, Anne or Anna will become my LAST ONE AND ONLY, just tell me you don't appreciate, savor the notion, I most certainly do, but I don't mean to make too much of this, in other words focus on this thing, this ONE THING to the exclusion of any and all others, still, erections in general or my particular erection cannot, will not be denied, although I've had better in the past, thicker, firmer and all in all more assertive, and then, yes, of course, I knew just what, in other words precisely what to do with them, more or less I mean, ah, the stories I could tell if I had the time, the inclination, the ENERGY, let me just say, assert the following, the kindness of strangers never a problem as far as my ERECTIONS OF THE PAST were concerned, in other words my tail or tale of the past was never one told by an idiot and SIGNIFYING NOTHING, now it's the reverse, yes, I'm almost sure, my current tail or tale very much one told by an idiot and SIGNIFYING NOTHING, I'm sure you'll agree, but it's pointless to pursue the matter any further, or any other matter for that matter, let's just say the sun still rises and sets just as my erections still rise and set, and let that be the end for the time being.

Finders keepers.
I hope I'm making my point.
Ah, but what clichéd expressions, what gaps in the past, one could

analyze one's past ad infinitum and still come up with nothing more than gaps filled in by hackneyed expressions, let's not, but was it always the same or always different, I only wish I knew, but yes, here's a question for you, does what mattered then still matter or what matters now already of SOME SIGNIFICANCE back then, 'Seek and ye shall find,' I'd like to say, but, no, I just can't, it no longer applies if it ever had, yes, just now I wet myself, yet again, I'm afraid there's no help for it, I refuse, yes, simply refuse to wear those so-called senior diapers Anne or Anna insists on, no sooner does she put them on than I tear them off the first chance I get, yes, LET THE PISS FLOW is my motto, and in spite of her serious doubts on the matter this has nothing, but absolutely nothing to do with her but everything with me, my remaining tenacity or love of life, if I may so boldly assert, exhibited, in fact contained in this unobstructed flow of piss, yes, 'Here I am and here I piss,' like a modern-day Luther facing his last, his final challenge, DEATH ITSELF of course, and if Anne or Anna or anyone else doesn't get it, well, it's not my role to enlighten them any more than I already am, all of us with our roles in life after all, whether it's pissing or cleaning up that piss, you see my point I think, we can no more shirk our roles than we can stop carrying on from one day to the next and the one after that, so long as our STRENGTH HOLDS OUT, and I only wish Ms. Boyer or Anne or Anna would understand and appreciate, complicating her job, her life the farthest thing from my mind, she must recognize my diminished and ever diminishing ways of expressing myself, thoughts, memories, even words very nearly shot to hell, in other words the PAST practically shot to hell and the present, ah, yes, only something of the EVER PRESENT remains, which in this particular instance is piss of course with its sheer physicality, its staggering simplicity, but I may well be pushing here in asking for this sort of understanding, just how much understanding a man, yes, even a dying man is entitled to is open to question, but here, here we go, just a few more drops and I'll be done, the flow of piss very like the flow of time in this, eventually, ah, EVENTUALLY they both cease and desist, in other words come to a DEFINITIVE END, I for one can hardly wait, 'Ah,' I'll sigh,' done with pissing, done with time, done with life itself,' ah, but not yet, you see what I'm getting at, NOT JUST YET, and if only Ms. Boyer or Anne or Anna would understand, yes, for the moment I'm asking for no more than this.

I don't know why they still let her in.

"No more visitors," I think I told them, whom, yes, staff, nurses, doctors, it really doesn't matter, but the last thing I want are these self-styled resurrectors, accusers of the past, what's done cannot be undone, as a matter of fact as I no longer clearly recall what was or wasn't done, the chances of its becoming undone is not even a remote possibility, but still they do come, manage to get in somehow, and then I'm in the awkward, the dreadful position of having to distinguish among them, in most, in nearly all of the cases I have to be informed in advance, "Your wife, Viktor," or, "A fellow musician," or more simply, "A friend," or even "Your best friend," truth is I no longer recall or do my best not to recall any friends or even a so-called best friend, and while he, whoever, may once have considered himself my best friend it doesn't follow that I ever considered him mine, although I just don't know, but for now it's my wife, my so-called last, Samantha as she keeps on insisting, although what she means to gain by this I simply don't know.

"Viktor, my love," she begins, and I wish she wouldn't.

And if you think this is amusing, it's not.

Not even close.

Yes, even her touch is odious to me, although this may not be the right word, no matter, I'll stick to it for the time being, but, "Viktor, my love," she starts and continues from there, and the very way she lays her hands, please note, both her hands on top of my one, induces a certain vertigo, motion sickness in me, in other words casts me adrift even though I'm doing my utmost, my very best to lie absolutely still in my bed, but, "Viktor, my love, how I wish I could trade places with you," or, "I only wish I could trade places with you," which aside from being meaningless is not in the least helpful, yes, people forever saying what they can't possibly mean or meaning what they can't express, I'm just not sure, and, here we go, her very smile, elegance, and what I can only call her attractive bearing something of an insult to me, her very presence nothing but a reinforcement, a reminder of the distance between us, in fact this woman, this so-called Samantha has always had, carried about these built-in distances no matter the time or place, what I saw in her, yes, something of a mystery but not one that I'm in any way anxious to solve, and, "I just hope you're comfortable, that they're treating you well," she continues, and still she doesn't ease, release the pressure of her two hands on top of my one, and, "Everyone," she goes on, "everyone's been asking about you, I tell them what I can, which isn't much of course, but I tell them you're putting up a brave struggle, that you're not the type to simply let go, to surrender without a fight," our eyes meet, part then meet again, although neither of us capable of even desirous of maintaining any lasting looks, "I am like the keeper of the gate, Viktor," she continues, "with your friends, colleagues and even your ex-lovers coming and going as they please, I haven't the strength or the courage to turn them away," I nod, what else, I simply nod, "they would much rather visit you , of course, but I tell them no, you need your strength, and at any rate you barely speak, about all you can do is listen now," Samantha, if that's who she is, gives my hand a little squeeze, most annoying I assure you, "I'm running interference for you, Viktor, as I have for most of our life together, I'm just grateful I'm a strong woman, which I basically am, because only a strong woman could have handled living with a man like you, and now, yes, even now only a strong woman can handle the past, your past engulfing me like a flood," tears, yes, those may well be tears in her eyes but I wisely refrain from looking more closely, from investigating to make sure, "but you can count on me, Viktor, you know that, I think you realized this from the start which is why you persisted, insisted on marrying me, for my part I was always skeptical, I don't have to tell you, I've always had my misgivings about becoming, being the wife of a man like you," ah, if only I could recall, it would certainly simplify matters, but, no, it might, it just might make them more difficult "how is it, Viktor, really, how is it that certain women willingly sacrifice themselves for certain men, no, I don't think I understand," she looks off into the distance as if seeking to find me there and not here, RIGHT HERE lying in front of her, "love, yes, perhaps love is the only explanation, although you and I both know that's much too simple an explanation, in fact no explanation at all, perhaps I was just running from things, running from myself, or, who knows, I may be just a masochist like everyone else I know," that smile again, yes, that annoying, irritating smile, "like everyone who's ever been associated with you, all your friends, your women so willing to sacrifice themselves for a man who was simply incapable of caring, of caring at a deep level I mean, oh, I'm not saying you never loved me or perhaps still do, not for me to say, but you never made me feel like your partner, do you understand, Viktor, never a sharer in your life," I resort to a coughing spell, half real, half fake, what other choice do I have, "but all that's water under the bridge, I mean there you are and here I am, I think that's all that matters now, and I'll keep coming, Viktor, no, nothing will keep me away because when you care for someone that's what you do, Viktor, I don't think you realize, you want to be with them for as much and for as long as you can, and I'd just wish you'd say something, anything at all, I get tired of listening to myself, of being the only one who has something, anything to say."

The window wide open.

A blessing really.

Birds and such, noises from the street.

"You're looking well, Samantha," I finally tell her. "Vibrant, beautiful. Really, a sight for sore eyes."

Which is not a lie, it most certainly is not, or just a partial one at worst.

But I could as easily have said, 'You're a sore for sight eyes,'

And perhaps should have.

I just don't know.

Does it matter?

What?

Anything, anything at all.

Does it still matter?

Ah, but what a time we had.

The plural, not the singular?

Yes, I don't see why not.

Because in this 'we' I include everyone I've ever known, had contact with or even just thought about, and men as well as women, please, let me be clear about this, the men as well as the women, in other words everyone who has ever affected my life and I theirs perhaps, in other words a Mozart, a Beethoven, a Mahler as well as my so-called lovers, friends, musical colleagues, what have you, and I don't see why I shouldn't include in this list perfect or near perfect strangers, people just hurriedly seen and once, please note, only once and then hidden, sheltered in some corner of the mind, I can only assume without the ability of actually, recalling, but all of them there or here or somewhere else, and there are days or perhaps just moments of certain days when I wish they could all gather around my bed, an impossible, a harrowing thought of course but still there are those moments, and then we, yes, WE could reminisce, reconsider, go over everything that has ever happened to us to the minutest details, and this from a man who most days can't even recall what he had for breakfast or lunch or whether the afternoon was sunny or cloudy, but I'm beginning to realize something, and, please, just let me say this, that in some very basic, elemental and even essential sense so-called LIFE is nothing but RELATIONSHIPS, bear with me, that unless it is related the single 'I' is not only useless but senseless as well, in other words it simply DOES NOT MAKE ANY SENSE, and I just hope you see where I'm headed with this, but all my life this single, solitary 'I' the only thing I ever truly recognized and perhaps even cared about, a harsh judgment, I know, but if not now, when, and in all my so-called contacts with others what else was I doing but looking for reflections of this single, solitary 'I,' no, there is no getting around, no whitewashing this single, this damning fact, and perhaps, I'm just saying, but perhaps that's the origin, the very nature of our original FALL, the consciousness of this single, solitary 'I' to the exclusion of everyone, everything else, and looked at in this light even my so-called music doomed to be unoriginal and second rate precisely because it was always EXCLUSIVE and never INCLUSIVE, unlike the music of a Mozart, a Beethoven and even a Mahler which at their best were both original and first rate precisely because they were INCLUSIVE AND NOT EXCLUSIVE, and my loves, my numerous affairs, all of them unoriginal and second rate precisely because they were always EXCLUSIVE and never INCLUSIVE, in other words have I ever seen the universal in the specific and the specific in the universal, although it may be a bit late, too late to ask this sort of question, but even if I've just administered a fairly high dose of morphine to my system the question still with a certain degree of legitimacy, in other words still valid above and beyond the morphine' s effects, but now this lovely numbness, drowsiness which may well negate everything I've been thinking, you see the problem I think, in other words tomorrow or the day after, and that's with or without the morphine, I may well come up with an entirely different analysis of why I WAS THE WAY I WAS or BECOME WHAT I'VE BECOME, I mean I just don't know, but for now this is it, please note, THIS IS IT, but I'm already drifting off, thank god, and soon there will be no need to make sense of this or of anything else for that matter.

I've already waited an hour for her.
And please don't ask who, it's not at all essential to the memory of that spring afternoon.
The waiting, you see, only my waiting essential.
A lovely April afternoon, like now I suppose, yes, precisely like now, although I mention this only in passing, it neither adds to nor detracts from that memory of the past, but I was waiting at this prearranged time and place, my outdoor table at this restaurant strategically located so that I would see her approach from a distance, yes, the more specific the details the better I think, but all of my life up to that point contained in that waiting, yes, I'm quite sure, and whether she would or would not show would determine the direction, the very course of the rest of my life, at least that's what I felt or at any rate told myself, needless to say she was MY ONE AND ONLY or the GRAND LOVE OF MY LIFE, then I mean, yes, exactly, then, and during that period of waiting I observed and thought, and, really, there was no difference, but thought and observed with an effortless ease in other words during that period of waiting I somehow managed to observe not only everyone and everything else but MYSELF as well, please note, for once the observer the observed and the observed the observer, I can't emphasize this enough, and it wasn't that I became all I observed, no, nothing as mystical, as ridiculous as that, but the observer and the observed were ONE, please, tell me you understand, or there was only OBSERVING and no OBSERVER, yes, better I think, and while there were some fleeting thoughts, of course, always some fleeting thoughts such as will she or won't she come and what will happen if she does or doesn't come, they were of little or no importance, I paid them no attention, yes, let me repeat, the WAITING all there was, all that mattered, yes, even though she was MY ONE AND ONLY or even the GRAND LOVE OF MY LIFE

at the time, yes, and even whether I would have my heart healed or broken did not seem to matter, I mean I could foresee either eventuality without any strong and therefore detrimental feelings, in fact, 'What will happen will happen, Viktor', I think I even said to myself, and perhaps, I'm just saying, but perhaps I even looked forward to having my heart healed or broken to an equal degree, either eventuality simply a part of LIFE, of every thing there ever was and would be, and the only important or interesting thing was how I would handle it, in other words how I would manage to CARRY ON, let me repeat, one eventuality no more or less intriguing than the other so long as I could continue to observe, keep tabs on my reactions afterwards, and in the end, ah, IN THE END I can't even recall whether she showed or not, in other words whether this became a brand new beginning, a continuation or simply the end of our so-called affair, the only thing that remains locked in my mind now is the period of waiting that contained all possibilities and therefore none in particular, and in that period of waiting I seemed most myself because I was no longer only myself, but, please, don't ask me to make this any clearer than I already have, in fact it's no longer as clear to me as when it was when the memory first asserted itself, becoming quite a blur in fact as does, is everything after a while, nothing to be done about that I'm afraid, no, NOTHING AT ALL.

Always the same.

Is it?

Yes, practically.

The same thoughts, the same memories, the same pains, the same room, sun, light, darkness, although not exactly, not entirely, some slight differences now and again which is what makes one continue, CARRY ON after all.

When there is no hope.

Do you understand?

WHEN THERE IS NO HOPE.

Although the absence of hope is not exactly hopelessness, and then there are the differences, the ever so slight differences from time to time.

Anything? Anything at all?

Yes.

Let's just focus on the most immediate, essential, on Ms. Boyer or Anne or Anna for argument's sake.

Mostly the same of course, from one week, day, even one hour to the next, but now and again some slight difference, I never fail to notice, appearance, gestures, words I'm talking about, no doubt the reactions to events in her OTHER LIFE, the one away from here I mean, but I never inquire, I never press, a man with just a single life, his last remaining life really has no right to question the still multiple lives of another, I think you'll agree, I certainly know my place, yes, that's the thing about the dying, they almost always know their places, although sometimes not, thank god, at any rate I can always read the signs of changes in Ms. Boyer's OTHER LIFE or LIVES, and at times I'm tempted, I must confess, to use those changes as starting points for changes in OUR JOINT LIFE, sounds ridiculous I know, but I think you know what I mean, and there are, have been occasions when just a single well intoned question might, mind you, just might do the trick, I'm thinking of something like, 'Anything the matter, Anne?' or Anna, or more simply, 'What' s wrong, Anne?' or Anna, or simpler still, 'Anne?' or Anna, I mean that just might serve as a catalyst of sorts, create a kind of opening that would work BOTH WAYS, I think you know what I mean, but so far I've resisted, kept this impulse in check, it's not at all certain that I'm in a state of body and mind to make the best or even a relatively good use of such an opening, I have in the past of course, on countless occasions, there is no surer way to a woman' s heart and mind than to entice her to unburden herself, in my experience women live to reveal, to unburden themselves whereas men do the opposite, they live merely to hide and in the process burden themselves, in general I'm talking about, although the simple rule about men with women and women with men is that all rules apply or none at all.

But Anne or Anna in a bit of a peculiar mood today, I only wish I were without pains, chills, fever, and those unpredictable dizzy spells, yes, then I could read those outward signs more clearly, the raised eyebrows, the slumped shoulders, the downward, but only slightly, turn of the lips, and from there hypothesize about the inner turmoil from her OTHER LIFE, and then, trust me, I could appreciate, sympathize and possibly penetrate, and that, please, would be to both our advantages, which of course she doesn't realize, no, no way she could, or I could simply start by saying the following, yes, I thought of another approach, 'Time is running out, Anne' or Anna, meaning not just for me, which is fairly obvious, but for her as well, because, after all, what are her torments, disturbances in her OTHER LIFE but manifestations of time and if time then they are sure to pass, in other words everything, all of us made of time stuff, what else, there should, there must be some way to get this across, yes, yes, except for one single and singular exception, the TWO OF US TOGETHER, ah, but how often I've tried a similar or even the same exact approach with other potential lovers in the past, in other words, 'Could it be you and me, Grace?' or Sarah, Louise, or Anne or Anna as in this particular case, this particular here and now, but the number of times really doesn't matter, it in no way negates that this, yes, that this particular time could REALLY BE IT, in other words that in, through and with time Anne or Anna and I could conceivably sail beyond time itself, certain physical obstacles, I don't think I need explain, but certain physical impediments not withstanding, and a single inkling of such a possibility might be enough to get us started, it just might, and then, oh, yes, THEN, everlasting, joy, bliss, whatever, although I myself hardly believe this, as a matter of fact I never have, but, still, no matter how unrealistic, one must hold out some sort of HOPE simply to carry on, you see the problem of course, I'm sure you do.

So.

Here I and there Anne or Anna, or there Anne or Anna and here I.

And, please, let me not focus on my chills, fever and dizzy spells, it's the last thing I want to do, just now I need all my powers of concentration, of sympathy to study Anne or Anna the way I've never studied another human being, another woman before, although I've tried, believe me, I have tried in the past, but, no, never with this urgency, this feeling of a last ditch effort, it's do or die as far as I'm concerned, or first DO and then, only then DIE, I am sure you can appreciate, in other words it's still LIFE before DEATH or just a bit more LIFE before the finality of DEATH, just tell me you understand, comprehend the importance of the issue at stake. I manage a smile.

I think I do, just about, in fact I'm fairly certain.

And this just as she bends, is bending right over me, checking one thing or another, but the opportunity too good to miss and in fact I do manage a smile.

And.

"Everything all right, Viktor?" she asks.

Ah, more than likely the thing intended to be a smile never quite blossoming, falling short in other words, understandable under the circumstances, my muscle control no longer what it once was, in fact the intended smile more of a grimace than a smile, yes, I'm quite sure, and where, bear with me, JUST WHERE is one of my vaunted or daunted or haunted erections, which of course would be a much more obvious, even definitive sign of my unbridled or perhaps just bridled desires than a mere smile could ever be, but, no, apparently my erections come and go as they please and not at all as I, in other words I can't simply resurrect them when the TIME IS RIGHT, and then it passes, the moment I mean, Anne or Anna moves on while I stay FIRMLY and USELESSLY PUT, and with IT, HER, ME all hope passes as well, and who knows when it will come again, the OPPORTUNITY I mean, HOPE I mean, and once more I'm back in the dark, relatively speaking, shut my eyes so I no longer have to see and hope and think but only imagine, that's it, you see, imagination the last refuge against the unspeakable, against DEATH.

Yes.

Here is what I tell myself.

Life, after all, of some significance.

And death?

No, of no significance whatever.

A healthy attitude I think.

Are you listening?

Although attitudes come and go, in other words it's one attitude one day or even hour and another, some other the next, good, bad, indifferent it hardly seems to make any difference, but when a good one comes along it's best to seize it, hang on to it as long as possible, LIFE OF SOME SIGNIFICANCE, and, again, I'm not talking of some overall, some universal significance, no, at this stage of my living, my dying I'd be the last one to attempt it, sell myself a bill of goods in the end at drastically reduced, at going out of business prices, no, throughout my life I've purchased all sorts of goods, some at regular, others at discounted and still others at highly inflated prices, and have they done me any good, near the end I mean, no, no good at all, because in the END all goods must be abandoned, discarded, I'm sure I'm not telling you anything you don't already know or at any rate suspect, one travels light near the end, that's it, so light in fact that there's NOTHING, please note, NOT A SINGLE THING one carries along, and then what remains, ah, terrific question, a certain occasional, fleeting attitude that LIFE IS OF SOME SIGNIFICANCE after all, and I mean for the living, strictly for the living because nothing, ABSOLUTELY NOTHING matters to the dead, and how to embrace, to make something of this, a bit of a problem all right, although, no, not a problem, one is beyond all so-called problems near the end, even dying no longer a problem, it will simply happen when it does, but while there is life, any sort of life, it must still be of SOME SIGNIFICANCE.

Here we go.

Visitors.

Yes.

I think by now you know my feelings, my absolute abhorrence of any and all visitors, all visitors simply messengers from the past, dragging with them all the useless baggage, the accumulated garbage of the past, I only wish I could think of another word, but, no, 'garbage' will have to do, but none of my so-called visitors ever in the immediate, the ever present, bear with me on this, all of them residents of the past which they shamelessly exhibit in an attempt to drag me back there as well, but it's too late, please, it's TOO LATE for me to be dragged anywhere at all, least of all the past, I'm no longer willing even if I were still able, I'm no longer willing to be dragged ANYWHERE AT ALL.

In other words here I am and here I'll stay, I absolutely refuse to be moved from this spot.

And still, and I just hope this is clear, there is, there remains some SIGNIFICANCE TO LIFE.

A squirrel.

Here we go.

Of all my visitors he or she, because I have no way of telling, but he or she remains my one and only welcome visitor, his first visit accidental, even something of a mistake perhaps, a simple hop from the limb of a tree to the window's ledge and then right through, right onto that chair by the window, and you should have seen his confusion, even panic that first time, he hardly knew which way to scurry, to scamper, to climb, the unfamiliar surroundings played havoc with his sense of direction, his very sense of self-preservation, yes, this very room nothing but an IMMEDIATE, an EVER PRESENT danger to his very existence, and I as well of course, this inert but still living body anchored to this bed, yes, I think it's safe to say that that first sight of me nearly scared him to death, I on the other hand was simply surprised, totally amazed at his sudden appearance, no matter, but it took him quite a bit of furious yet futile attempts to escape, to find his way back out before he exhausted himself and settled down on top of that dresser, and, "It's all right," I think I told him, "don't worry, everything will be all right," and eventually, no, I don't know how long, my sense of time truly shot to hell, but eventually he calmed himself and realized how easy it was to find his way to the open window, and then he was gone, but this, you see, this for me was that some SIGNIFICANCE TO LIFE I've been talking about, and afterwards, yes, of course, AFTERWARDS I asked Anne or Anna for some nuts without in any way explaining, but just for some nuts to place on the windowsill in a vain attempt to make possible, to bring about a second visit, but since that first visit was sheer chance, pure accident I think I knew that it would never occur again, ONCE AND ONCE ONLY, you see, and all that is very much in keeping with that slight, even ridiculous SIGNIFICANCE TO LIFE, but, still, one hopes of course, and actually, eventually a second, third, and even a fourth visit did occur, but, no, nothing like that first which was sheer chance and pure accident, but I'm growing tired, losing the thread, the point of my story, unless, ah, yes, it's that slight SIGNIFICANCE TO LIFE, but let's let it go, yes, it's best to let it all go for now.

And then, yes.
Something happens.
Always, always something no matter how slight, insignificant, but

something always does happen, which is how one continues, keeps going after all.

What?

Ah, not that easy to say.

The sun rising and setting, but we've covered that before, and the leaves, yes, already some leaves on the trees, moving, swaying, fibrillating, lovely word that, or perfectly still depending, breeze or no breeze, wind or no wind, but we must move on, yes, list some other things as well, not always easy, and Ms. Boyer, yes, let's continue, coming and going, moving to and fro, a pleasant sight although not always, no, certainly not always but more often than not I'd say, and sometimes, yes, let me just add, sometimes in the middle of the night, here we go, entering and exiting my dreams, I hardly know myself, and in the night or in my dreams we appear a perfect match, and I say this without any hesitation or just a slight one perhaps, but let's just say she knows her way about my dreams as well as I do myself, enters and inhabits them the way I do myself, expands, stretches them in different directions although the directions of no consequence and neither is time itself of course, my dreams exist well beyond the BOUNDARIES OF TIME, I, we make sure, although it's confusing, in other words deceptive to say 'my dreams', they're as much hers as they are mine, we create them together with now she, now I taking the initiative, the upper hand as it were, 'You see how simple, how easy?' one of us will remark and the other will nod, smile or the other way around, and in the dream or dreams, ah, but how satisfying, fulfilling to continue in this fashion, but in the dream neither of us with any links, ties to either the past or the future, that follows, of course it does, from the TIMELESS TIME we inhabit, in other words neither of us with any of the burdens imposed by time, both of us entirely, completely, wholly OURSELVES, although this notion of OURSELVES a tricky one, both of us as light as air or even lighter, I mean imagine a snowflake, yes, just a single snowflake at the very moment it melts in the palm of your hand, I'm just trying to give you some idea, and our movements the same, light, ephemeral and entirely without ANY EFFORT, and, 'Isn't it curious, amazing,' one of us will say, it hardly matters who, but, 'isn't it curious, amazing how all my life I've been searching for you, only to find you here and now, in a dream, at the very edge of death,' but of course in the dream we don't think of it as a 'dream' , no, something else, something entirely different, and, yes, it would be dreadful to quit, to stop now, yes, let's just hope I have the strength to continue as I've begun, but Anne or Anna, no, I'll just call her Anna now, from now on she'll always and only be 'Anna' to me, but Anna approaches from above while I remain below, although the other way works just as well, she draws near, embraces, clasps, and then we become or simply ARE ONE, and I just hope you realize the importance, the unqualified significance of this, WE ARE ONE, we simply move in and through each other as though it were the most natural thing in the world, the physical still the physical of course, I'm not saying, but the physical no longer any sort of obstacle, and, 'Have you always loved me?' she asks or I, and, 'Yes, always, ever since time began or ended,' and as for the rest, no, here is where we move beyond even the realms of imagination, in other words not even imagination can encompass, do it justice.

I wake.
Sweat soaked, dream soaked, imagination soaked.
I wake.
Anna bending over me.
"You're burning up. The fever dangerously high."
Yes.
Erection?
No, useless to talk of an erection now.
The high fever her only concern and should be mine as well.
Please note the tense, the subjunctive.
Important I think.
"Get you into a cold tub as fast as we can."
I'm in no position to argue, to object.
Others show.
They break the spell, the fever, much more effectively than the cold tub ever will.

So much is asked of us in life.
In death?
No, nothing at all.

But so much is asked of us in life, by others, by ourselves that it's impossible to measure, to fulfill.

Is it important?

But in life we never, please listen, we NEVER come up to our own or others' expectations, the few of us who do, the Mozarts, the Beethovens, the Mahlers do so through some gift, some miracle of nature perhaps, no, I have never clearly understood, but the Mozarts, the Beethovens, the Mahlers fulfill their own and others' expectations as much in spite of as because of who and what they are, yes, it's in their music, only in their music that they truly become a Mozart, a Beethoven or a Mahler, in other words the Mozart, the Beethoven, the Mahler we know and love, but otherwise no, they are confused, abandoned, lost souls the same as the rest of us, yes, the only difference is that they, a Mozart, a Beethoven, a Mahler somehow managed to answer the CALL, to fulfill whatever was demanded of them or whatever they demanded of themselves, yes, I think that's right, a call, please listen, I never clearly heard in my life, or if I did, ah, that obnoxious 'if', I only partially, half-heartedly responded, yes, all you have to do is listen to my so-called music, my so-called achievements and compare it to their UNQUESTIONABLE MASTERPIECES, as a matter of fact as a musician I lived my life as an impostor, tell me you understand, and perhaps my other life or lives as well, in other words lived it or them as an IMPOSTOR as well, and whatever satisfaction or happiness I attained they were the satisfaction and happiness of an IMPOSTOR, and all this because I never heard or felt the CALL, and never, please note, NEVER demanded anything extraordinary of myself or had others demand it of me, in other words everything I demanded of myself or others demanded of me was of a mundane and ordinary quality, and so, listen, my life or lives, musical and otherwise, became, was and still is a life or lives of little or no CONSEQUENCE, but perhaps, PERHAPS this is all right at or near the end when life demands NOTHING more of us than our deaths, when lives of little or no CONSEQUENCE are no longer distinguishable from lives that have made a TREMENDOUS DIFFERENCE, I mean I just don't know, and this, yes, listen, this is how life makes LOSERS of us all in the end, and in this sense, ah, but how this argument meanders, but in this sense those who have been LOSERS all along are ahead of the game in the end, because one loss, even if the ultimate one, but one loss more or less can or should hardly matter to them, yes, but the thing is IT STILL DOES, because near the end it's still not too late to demand something, some EXTRAORDINARY SOMETHING of oneself, I mean a loser in life still has a chance to die as something other than a loser in the end, but don't mind me, once again I'm simply off and running without any goal or direction, the deterioration of the mind fully in keeping with the increasing deterioration of the body, so let's just let it go, pay it as little attention as possible.

Ah, spring.
Yes, I'm quite sure.
I mean I can read most if not all the signs, although just now I don't feel like elaborating, but spring let's just say, and if anyone ever needed convincing of the cyclical nature of time, well, here it is, SPRING, in other words birth, death and rebirth, although to apply this to a personal level, no, I don't think I'm capable, but, 'To die in spring, Viktor,' I occasionally tell myself and simply let it go at that, and, here we go, Anna with a bit of a spring to her walk unless I'm very much mistaken, Anna who in spite of her incredibly straight bearing and purposeful locomotion can appear to shuffle now and again, now with a definite spring to her walk, and her cheeks flushed, naturally not unnaturally, in other words not the result of any makeup which I know she abhors but of something else, and, yes, "Breathe deeply," she even advised the other morning, and this in spite of my collapsing or already collapsed lung, the left I think, and once again I started thinking, imagining, saying things like, 'Could it be Anna and me?' to myself, I could hardly help it, and then, yes, we actually managed a walk through the garden, although she of course managed infinitely better than I, it goes without saying, but I clung, hung in, I was not about to let go, in other words it was definitely a walk of sorts, and, let me tell you, the very boundaries of life and death, although they were merely the boundaries of that garden, appeared to be shifting then, our own boundaries as well, bear with me, now and again we approached the gate which both was and wasn't a gate, neither of us sure, but with just a flick of the finger we could have easily opened it and passed right through, although we didn't, no, I don't

think we found it necessary, and it was in this fashion that we passed into spring, although 'passed' too weak a verb, I leave it to you to think of a better one, 'cut', yes, perhaps, cut into spring, and it worked both ways of course, as we cut into spring, spring most certainly cut into us, the sights, the sounds, the smells, and now and again I stopped, made Anna stop to touch a branch, a twig, a leaf, and amazing how that branch, that twig, that leaf cut right through me, we moved on, the garden, which from my window always appeared confined, limited, appeared endless now, and while we may have been moving around in circles, seeing the same branches, twigs, perhaps even leaves over and over again it simply DID NOT MATTER, Anna held me by the crook of the arm or was it I clinging to her, no, I don't recall, but at some point, ah, if only I could be clear about the specific moment, but at some point I managed to pull ahead, stop and turn around, trust me, no INCONSEQUENTIAL ACT, it took all my reserves of strength, and then I approached, moved towards Anna, the distance no more than two or three steps but, oh, what steps they were, and then I reached out and embraced, yes, I'm almost sure, placed my arms about her the way any ordinary man might place his arms about an ordinary woman, please, note the adjective, ORDINARY, important I think, and then, dare I say it, pulled her close, ah, but this may be no more than wishful thinking after the fact, but IT MIGHT NOT, and, here we go, she didn't object, made absolutely no effort to back off, to free herself, and then, ah, yes, an erection, MY ERECTION, perfectly reasonable under the circumstances, in other words fully in keeping with our penetration of spring, she felt it of course, no way she couldn't have, yes, she even remarked on it, something like, "Does this mean what I think it means?" although, please, you mustn't hold me to this, the embrace, the erection quite sufficient without any need for words, yes, I'd be the first to negate, to sail beyond words at a moment like that, I could go on, did perhaps, but, no, a man in my situation must recognize where reality ends and fantasy begins, not easy of course, ah, but this is getting complicated, much more complicated than I originally intended, yes, let's just say we stood there for a spell without placing any limitations on the lapse or elapse of time, and then, what, no, I'm not sure, moved on I can only suppose, continued with our grand circle route of spring, and that's ENOUGH I think, it has to be, given the ridiculous, the faulty nature of memory, but SPRING, you see, which took both of us by surprise, and that's enough.

The gaps.

Yes, let's go on.

But all the gaps in memory, in time, and I hardly distinguish between the two, but all the intentional or unintentional gaps, all of us escape artists when it comes to memory, to time, yes, there's nothing we like better than to escape both memory and time, not possible of course, so we settle for gaps to facilitate our flight, yes, in the end we want nothing but reckless adventures that have nothing to do with either memory or time, not possible of course, the gaps all we have and must make the most of.

In other words our memories selective, remember what we must and avoid what we can, it's absolutely essential, necessary for our survival in the present.

I sat absolutely still.

Yes, I'll go on.

But I sat absolutely still, her idea not mine, "Promise me, Viktor, promise you won't budge," she, who, no, it no longer matters, but SHE with some bizarre notions, and she wasn't MY ONE AND ONLY or the GRAND LOVE of my life, of this I'm quite sure, no, not even at the time, but I was attracted by her curious ideas, her bizarre notions, I readily admit, she, yes, all SHE needed was an audience and I both willingly and readily accepted the role, "You move, Viktor, and you'll never but never see me again," which I didn't at any rate, but of which, no, I had no idea at the time, I sat fully clothed on the floor while she undressed by the foot of her bed, she took her time of course, it goes without saying, SHE in full control of time and of everything that passed or didn't between us, and she was quite a bit younger than I at the time or the other way around, in other words I young and she old, but that, you see, that difference in personal time no longer of any consequence, yes, and not even then perhaps, in other words we inhabited the same exact time then as well as now, in memory I mean, but it was also clear or she made it absolutely clear that nothing of any physical, sexual nature would pass between us, that she would simply PERFORM and I OBSERVE, it somehow served her purposes at the time and mine as well, but once fully naked, and here again the passing or passage of time beyond my exact recollection, but once fully naked she sat with her legs spread on the edge of the bed, and eventually, please note, EVENTUALLY both her eyes and mine focused on her light or dark or golden triangle, oh, I only wish I could infallibly recall, I mean have the very physicality of that appearance possess me now the way it did then, yes, and it was nothing less than a REDUCTIO AD ABSURDUM or PUDENDUM then, in other words she became her light or dark or golden triangle then and I the same, the rest of the world, please note, all the REST OF THE WORLD disappearing into her light or dark or golden triangle, ah, but she was quite an artist, in fact a magician, her hands, her fingers touched, explored and gently spread while mine remained firmly and permanently locked in my lap, and throughout all this, time I mean, performer as well as observer equally essential, in fact this, listen, NONE OF THIS would have worked without the presence of both the performer and the observer, no, I can't emphasize this enough, eventually, yes, in time and with time her fingers with lives of their own, their quickening movements at once purposeful and erratic, but, no, in time and with time the fingers of one hand, the left I think, spreading and holding while those of the other rapidly flapping, fluttering like butterfly wings, which is what I both thought and felt at the time or just now perhaps, ah, but what a. journey, what an adventure this seemingly simple activity turned out to be for both the performer and the observer I needn't add, and talk about your gaps, your escapes, none more efficient, more intoxicating, in other words no movement superfluous, none wasted, and then the cry or cries, single or several although I prefer a single, unaccompanied one of satisfaction like a single note fully possessed, sustained and held, no doubt it's the musician in me, and then the denouement of course although my recollection of this no longer to be trusted, but it's that single note fully possessed and sustained that held me then even as it does now, curious how it now blends with, melts into all the noises from the street and down the corridor while still, you see, STILL rising above, individual, unique and perhaps, I'm just suggesting, EVERLASTING, although that particular concept impossible to encompass, make sense of, but beyond the BOUNDARIES OF TIME let's just say, that single note held and sustained, but I have no wish to take this any further, already taken it too far for all the good it does a man in my condition.

Let's see.

Seeing, hearing, smelling, touching.

Nothing what it should be or was even a month or a week ago. I'm simply categorizing, disclosing.

And tasting?

The same, I'm afraid.

What else?

Breathing?

No, don't get me started.

When a man struggles for the very breath of life, not always but often enough, all other struggles pale in comparison.

Ah, but it gets better or worse, believe me, it does.

Words and ideas no longer with their wonted and wanted clarity.

Do you understand?

But throughout our lives there are words and ideas, and the two nearly if not exactly the same, I won't quibble, but for the most part we live our lives through words and ideas, skip across the swift current of time by the steppingstones of words and ideas, and if you think I'm merely stipulating here, no, think again, in fact every notion of so-called clarity we think we possess comes to us through words and ideas, and then, yes, suddenly or gradually, and I'm in no position to say, but suddenly or gradually the words and ideas turn on us or we on them, hard to say, but the words and ideas begin to fade and or diminish and or exchange identities, please, do your best to follow, in other words they masquerade, confuse and effectively hide themselves, yes, at or near the end it's nothing but a game of HIDE AND SEEK with words and ideas, and then, yes, again gradually or suddenly we begin to realize that the importance, all the prior importance we placed on words and ideas were not only sadly but even dangerously mistaken, because if words, if ideas were or had been all that important they would not now mislead, confuse and altogether turn on us, in other words life still goes on, OUR LIVES STILL CONTINUE but now without the aid of so-called words and ideas, and then the accompanying recognition, again, sudden or gradual, that all along, ALL OUR LIVES in other words, words and ideas far from having been aids have been nothing but OBSTACLES, that life, the very heart, soul and essence of OUR LIVES is to be found somewhere beyond words and ideas, I mean if anywhere at all, and then, yes, we become naked to and for ourselves, we may still pretend to be fully dressed but in fact we are standing in front of a mirror where only our nakedness is reflected, and it's in that nakedness, that vulnerability, that loss that we truly recognize ourselves, in other words come face to face with someone who is nothing but nakedness, loss and vulnerability, nothing but a bundle of pains and losses of sight, hearing, touching, smelling and so on, but, no, I have no wish to end on a strictly negative note, although at this stage nothing would be simpler, more convenient, but no, in spite of all these pains, losses and betrayals by words and ideas something, here we go, SOME SOMETHING of life still remains, and even if it isn't our individual, our personal lives, no, SOMETHING OF LIFE ITSELF still remains, but·don't press me on this, don't ask me to explain any further, to go any deeper than this, I, we, none of us capable, just take it on faith if you must, or don't, at this stage it really doesn't matter to me.

Someone named Sylvia I'm informed.
But should I must I go on?
Indeed, I don't see where I have a choice.
But yet another visitor announced, ah, but will the past never tire of trying to catch up with me, of pulling me back where I no longer reside, but the name pleasant enough as is the person, yes, at last someone kind, pleasant and perhaps even caring, although, no, I have absolutely no recollection of either the name or the person, nor do I wish to, but she appears to be fully there in her dark eyes and I as well perhaps, that is someone both like and unlike me in the past, and for once, I don't know why, but for once I decide to play this game of recollection, that is fake a memory that's no longer mine to possess, easier, simpler this way, and, "It's so wonderful to see you," she begins or ends or both, and her verbs, adverbs and adjectives lovingly multiplied as she continues, although she raises some tricky, thorny questions, can't be helped I suppose, here, I'll just cite one example, "Have I meant as much to you as you have to me?" yes, that'll do

I think, and then, playing the game, I of course reply to her question with a well chosen one of my own, "But how can you ask that?" sufficient, yes, and even more than for our so-called dialogue, which, just as I hoped, turns into a monologue by and by, and, "Do you remember the night, the stars?" she asks, which is rhetorical, thank god, just an intro to her account of that one, that single night we spent together, out of doors I can only assume, yes, on a hill or in some field somewhere, either will do, and the temperature mild and the visibility limitless, yes, let's just say for argument's sake, and for some reason the stars or assorted heavenly bodies of some significance or even an OVERRIDING IMPORTANCE, "The vastness overwhelming," she goes on, "and I felt quite literally lost, I mean all that space and stuff, and you, of course, I was lost in you as well, and the two somehow merged, I think for you as well, I mean they felt the same, being lost in all that space and in you, and then, and this may surprise you, Viktor, but then I thought, 'Remember this night, everything about this night because it will never, never ever happen like this again,' and in retrospect I was proved right of course, because after that night my life went in one direction and yours in another, ah, but what happens to us, Viktor, what happens to all our lives in the end," she studies me with her dark eyes, and, whether I like it or not, I find myself, caught, trapped, reflected in those dark mirrors, "but now, even right now I can't think of that night without thinking of those stars, conjuring up those stars that were inside me just as you were, and I'll tell you something, Viktor, may I, if I would have died on the spot, I mean right there with the stars and you inside me it would have been all right, in fact I often imagine I had, that you and I were both born and died that particular night, and that the rest, all the rest of our lives were simply lived in memory of that night, the mind plays funny tricks if we let it, but you must think me some kind of idiotic goose, you may not even recall that night or recall it the way I do, but when I heard about you I knew I had to come if only to tell you how clearly, how vividly I recalled that night, and also to let you know that as far as dying and death are concerned you have nothing to worry about because both of us have already died that night, died the moment we were born, and that I, we inhabited this immense space then which we never would again, and what better way to be born and to die than in the very immensity of space, and even though this may not make any sense to you, I can tell by the way you're looking at me that it probably doesn't, I simply had to come to let you know, to bring you this gift instead of the usual candy or flowers, although maybe I shouldn't have, just bring you some flowers and be done with it, recollect, remember, say nothing at all."

And then she is gone.

Or I am.

I shut my eyes, yes, lately I've been able to keep them open only for limited lengths of time, sooner or later the need, the irresistible urge in fact to escape, to disappear into darkness, and then when I open them again she, SYLVIA is gone as though she had never come, never even existed, and then, yes, once again I have a hard time distinguishing between the real and the imaginary, and then this great, this overwhelming sadness at not being able to recall, to REMEMBER exactly the way she had, and I ring for Anna to try to straighten out matters, whether in fact I did or didn't have a visitor just now, and, "Yes, of course," she smiles, "an older woman but extremely well preserved," and when I press for more, try to find out what if anything passed between us, Anna merely shrugs her shoulders, "No, as far as I could tell, hear, nothing much was said, she simply sat here for a spell and kept you silent company," and once again I shut my eyes to seek the safety, the security of darkness, because by now darkness more familiar to me than anything else, in fact everything occurring outside that haven of darkness simply confusing, testing me to the limit.

Yes.

This annoying change of identities.

My own, Anna's, and everyone, everything else's.

Animate as well as inanimate.

For example a chair just a chair one minute but the windowsill, the table and even the wall the next, or a pen, the simplest of objects turning into a thermometer, a tube, a stethoscope. when I'm not or even as I'm LOOKING, in other words under my very scrutinizing gaze, in other words my vision, my primary sense no longer to be trusted, or perhaps people as well as objects no longer to be trusted, they seem incapable of maintaining, guarding their identities, in fact, "Anna, are you sure you are who you are?" I asked the other afternoon, she took it as some sort of joke although it was nothing of the sort, and, "Here," she finally said, "see, feel for yourself," and extended her arm for me to touch and perhaps to squeeze, but this proved nothing of course, it was simply a futile, a useless exercise, the minute she turned around, backed off she turned into this immense, this scraggly alley cat, yes, "Anna, please don't play games with me," I even whispered, but, no, she first slithered than scampered across the floor, and she must have realized, although I don't know how she could have, but somehow she must have known that I've always harbored this deathly fear of cats, in fact, yes, only while composing were felines completely absent from my mind, and while a part of me recognizes that these apparitions, these changes of identities are nothing more than the effects or side effects of several new drugs they are trying out on me, yes, in some vain attempt to prolong my so-called precarious existence, another part, no, another part counsels that THINGS HAVE ALWAYS BEEN THIS WAY, that people and objects forever change identities, that the very nature of existence is one of PERPETUALLY CHANGING IDENTITIES, only we in our uncertainty, fear or even so-called wisdom choose not to see, to simply disregard, in other words we hardly ever dare come face to face with the naked truth, which is the truth of CHANGE and not at all the STABILITY, the SOLIDITY we manufacture for ourselves, in fact face to face with CHANGE, with the constantly shifting modes of existence we don't think we could continue, carry on, and of all our beliefs this the firmest perhaps, that we somehow need to manufacture a reality we can cope with, in other words one suitable to our CONTINUED SURVIVAL, but that reality is nothing but a fake, a sham as certain great, perhaps even magnificent composers fully realized, as the Mozarts, the Beethovens and the Mahlers of this world fully realized, their inimitable masterpieces born of and fully mirroring the unstoppable CHANGES of our EXISTENCE, which is why in their music they stood head and shoulders above all others while in their lives they were as miserable, confused and lost as everyone else, but once again I'm simply getting carried away, starting with one thing only to wind up with something else, or heading out in one direction only to wind up somewhere else, and perhaps it's always been this way, in other words not just now as a result of my illnesses and exotic drugs used to combat them, yes, and this is why, precisely, my so-called music never soared above the ordinary, the mundane, the fake to mirror something of the ESSENCE OF LIFE which is nothing more than change after all, and, while my logic may be faulty, I think I'm on to something, the feeling nearly impossible to deny, to escape, these changes, this constant shifting of identities surround me now the way they never have before, tree trunks turning into poles, their branches into synapses of nerves, and their leaves, please note, into swift moving clouds that NEVER touch the earth, and birds in flight, ah, but must I continue, but birds in flight into musical notations that attach themselves uncertainly to the ceiling above my head, but all this is becoming too much, exhilarating as well as exhausting, one of those days no doubt where MISTAKES have been made about both the type as well as the dosage of my medication, Anna to blame of course, yes, who else, but just now I'm afraid to ring for her, afraid of further complicating matters, she might just show as some furry beast or slimy creature, there is really no telling, and just now I feel incapable of handling one of her countless apparitions, it's an impossible predicament to be sure, but there is nothing, really NOTHING TO BE DONE.

Slim-legged.
Here we go.
Ah, but how the ideas still come and go, please note, the select memories, IMAGES as if I had nothing to do with them but they everything with me, we'll let that go, but once, you see, how attracted once to slim-legged women, although the thick-legged variety also of some interest but now, RIGHT NOW the images of thin-legged women or even just one, a particular woman, here we go, but I was drawn to her as if to a magnet, although at this distance in time it's nearly impossible to convey the allure, the attraction, the pull, yes, let's just say that in those days the sight of a slim-legged woman sufficient to arrest, to stop me dead in my tracks, at any rate the sight of this particular slim-legged woman, I had no choice of course, I simply had to follow her and improvise some means of making her acquaintance, yes, in this I was an able, perhaps even gifted improviser, and it's a shame, really, that the same cannot be said of my so-called music where my improvisational skills were woefully inadequate, at any rate nothing approaching a Mozart's or a Beethoven's, no matter, but, please,

keep me on track, at this questionable stage of my life it's essential that I stay on track, maintain some sort of focus, so, based solely on the sight of her slim legs I followed this woman, this particular woman, because as far as I was concerned everything about this woman was held and reflected by the sight of her slim legs, I must have been in my early twenties then but even my mid or late thirties or forties a possibility, no, that's not at issue here, the sensual, you see, only the sensual at issue here, yes, as far as I recall I have always been driven by the sensual to the near exclusion of everything else, but perhaps it's the 'sensuous', but, no, it won' t do to quibble over something like this, yes, let's just say I followed her and in time and with time I had her exactly where I wanted her, ah, but in those days I was not only an ordinary, a so-called run-of-the-mill lover, no, I fancied myself a highly accomplished explorer, perhaps even scientist, researcher of love, and then, yes, just then slim legged women constituted my special area of interest, but it goes without saying, although I feel obliged to do so, that this particular woman, in fact all women became full-fledged partners in my exploratory activities, in other words she, they, none of them ever treated as mere inert objects of study, none of them ever left behind, ah, if I had only devoted just a fraction of my amorous energies to my so-called compositions, but, no, why bring this up now, there is nothing to be gained, I'll go on, her slim legs were the means as well as the end back then, although, yes, in time and with time I unerringly worked my way to other parts of her body, explored, studied, in fact penetrated other parts of her body, but, no, without the stimulus, the catalyst of her slim legs none of this would have been possible, in fact without her thin legs it's more than likely that our encounter would never have taken place or if it had it would have merely turned into a mundane and highly forgettable sexual one, which THIS WASN'T, I only hope I'm making this clear, yes, as far as my amorous activities of the past are concerned there is way too much room for misunderstandings, misconceptions, but this was no mere sexual encounter, the role, the importance of slim-legged women to me at the time cannot be overestimated, but let me finish while I'm ahead or behind or on bottom or on top, it's best I think.

One, two, three.

Or four, five, six.

Or seven, eight, nine.

And ten.

Yes.

I occasionally count to myself as a way of keeping track of time or of keeping things, certain things, clear in my head, neither of which is entirely possible, in fact this activity something of a useless, meaningless exercise, I don't know who recommended it, Anna, yes, Anna perhaps.

Yes.

"Why don't you count to yourself?" she may have said during one of her lengthier examinations, yes, to take my mind off the sight of my wasting and wasted body or, and this is the explanation I favor, to keep my member, in other words my cock from rising to its once willful and glorious assertion, ah, I only wish, but what a lovely act of disobedience that would be to the PROPER NATURE of things or even the sheer PASSAGE OF TIME, in other words a challenge not to be lightly disregarded, in fact under my limited and limiting circumstances the most visible and effective, and effective because visible, challenge I can imagine.

And where would I, where would we go from there?

A hell of a question.

In fact certain days or certain hours of my days filled with nothing but teasing, annoying, in other words impossible questions, they accumulate like buds on trees or birds on the wing, and, 'Finally,' I even sigh to myself, yes, 'finally some terrific, some impossible questions,' and terrific because they are so impossible, in other words unanswerable, and it occurs to me, just now I mean, that all the greats, composers I'm talking about, set out to answer impossible questions or to challenge themselves with impossible questions, and even though they realized from the start that those questions were impossible because unanswerable, the very CHALLENGE of those questions became the substance of their MUSIC, whereas my music, I'm just saying, lacked any sort of similar substance, but that's neither here nor there, hardly worth bringing up, yes, let's say that now, RIGHT NOW those impossible questions accumulate in my head, perhaps I should keep tabs, list them as they appear, no, a simple count quite sufficient, in other words question one, two, three, four and so on, yes, Anna may have been on to something when she advised me to stick to numbers, to do nothing more than count, a way of dealing with things for sure, of reducing the activities of the mind to the absolute minimum, five, six, seven, eight and so on, yes, it doesn't do to get carried away at this last, this final, this ridiculous stage of my life, nine, ten, eleven, twelve, the only safety, certainty in numbers then, embrace, hold on to numbers to the exclusion of everything else, and in spite of the sheer lunacy and or hypocrisy of the endeavor I'll give it a shot, what have I got to lose, let me move among numbers then as if through some thick vegetation, the chances of finding my way no worse than through any other approach.

But kidding.

Yes.

Anna may have been kidding after all.

Some examples.

Yes.

I don't see why not.

But some examples of those impossible questions we were talking about.

Where am I?

Yes, terrific in its way once one digs past all the obvious, the facile responses.

This bed, this room, this hospital, these grounds, this city and so on practically ad infinitum, but, no, not quite infinitum because sooner or later one is forced to stop, runs out of geographical and even psychological landmarks, and then the true meaning, the very IMPOSSIBILITY of the question asserts itself, in fact it shines like a beacon in the darkness, WHERE AM I, and I just hope I'm conveying something with this, yes, something, anything at all.

Or how long have I been here?

And, again, we mustn't be deceived by the simplest and most readily available tools of measurement, days, hours, minutes, seconds and so on, their value entirely relative and even fictitious, in other words who's to say an hour is longer than a minute or a minute than a second, it's all up to the OBSERVER in the end whose only points of reference are what he thinks, feels and imagines, you see the difficulty I'm sure, and once one gets past all these initial and practically useless responses the question still looms, hovers like a storm cloud in the late afternoon sky, HOW LONG HAVE I BEEN HERE, and with this question the very nature of time comes under scrutiny, in other words what time does and doesn't do to our physical and mental being, or we to it, in fact, listen, TIME can hardly be separated from who and what we are at any particular stage, moment of our lives, here we go, in fact we are TIME STUFF, nothing more or less, although we'd like to think otherwise, desperately hope otherwise, but being TIME ITSELF the very measurement of time and or its comprehension something beyond the scope of our abilities, and I just hope I'm not getting entangled, confused in this meandering argument, if that's what it is, and even though time constitutes us it still escapes us in the end, or we it, ah, if I could only be sure, but all I'm saying is that a question like HOW LONG HAVE I BEEN HERE simply doesn't make any sense or if it does it's one of those impossible, unanswerable, in other words magnificent questions, number six or seven or eight, I'm not sure, but let's let it go, TIME and all the rest and focus on something more pressing, more immediate, the COLOR YELLOW for example, how it engulfs, seizes and captures, it's the most obvious and visible of all the colors, take just the yellow of the sun or of spring itself or of my skin certain early or late afternoons, in time and with time the world will end not in red or black or even white but in all-en-folding, all-consuming yellow, and that can't be too soon for me, although tomorrow I may feel different, but for now I wish nothing but to disappear, to become YELLOW in fact, a blazing sun on its way to its predestined extinction, from the very moment of its birth if we don't allow ourselves to be caught in the immensity, the impossibility of TIME ITSELF.

'After me the deluge.'
Lovely sentiment that.
But what deluge?
No, it won't matter to me by then, but the deluge of life left behind let's just say, or all my loves or all things done or left undone, my ridicu-lous music of course which is not destined to survive me or survive me by no more than a few years or decades at most, in other words I have no

expectation of surviving, living on in any form or fashion, for the briefest period of time in the minds of a select few perhaps, as a matter of fact, "Will you think of me after I'm gone?" I asked Anna the other day, or perhaps it was, "What will you think of me after I'm gone?" she made a face, one of her many to show annoyance as well as contempt perhaps, for someone so accustomed to death what else but annoyance and contempt at a question like that, in fact, "Easy come, easy go," she smiled after a while which I was free to interpret any way I chose, but I persisted, pushed on, I had no intention of letting her off the hook, "Ah, but Anna, you'll regret our not having taken the time to make some beautiful music together," which coming from a dying, a mediocre musician was not without its element of humor you must admit, Anna fixed me in her gaze, she did that at least, and, "Yes, perhaps if we had met years, decades ago," she replied, but I had a ready comeback for that, "Carpe diem, Anna," I whispered, gurgled, "carpe diem," the Latin for emphasis, her eyes, her hair darker then than on any previous occasion, or perhaps lighter, I only wish I could be certain, let me just say this though, she did bend over to stroke me above and even below my blanket, although, once again, certainty as to this last eludes me, and then, ah, here we go, "You're not who you pretend to be, are you?" she looked down, and, I must say, this took me by surprise, I wasn't aware of pretending just then although, as I've been pretending most of my life, this wasn't entirely out of the question, "All the same, all the same," I tried to recover, "you'll come to me one night when both you and I least expect it," and then, yes, just then an image, a fleeting vision of Anna on top and riding me to my VERY DEATH, and she must have read something of this on my face because, please listen, she said, 'Trust me, fucking is not all it's cracked up to be,' which was not only an unusual but an amazing thing for her to have said, the substance as well as the choice of words I'm talking about, I mean this was an Anna I simply didn't recognize or only wished to, and, "Oh, but Anna," I think I whispered, I may well have, and she, but I no longer recall how I, she, we continued after that, I mean I both do and don't, or in ways that matter I do or the other way around, let's just say that that morning or afternoon or at that PARTICULAR MOMENT light flooded the room, yellow I'd like to say, yes, why not, YELLOW, and that in that embracing, all-enfolding YELLOW we made love, ah, but how I'm reaching

here, but it's not, no, certainly not beyond the realms of possibility, or
within, yes, just barely within, the details sketchy though, how could they
be otherwise, I mean here or there you have or had a dying man, a wreck
although with something of a questionable erection, and here or there a
most proper or improper nurse, in other words fully alive, and I only wish
I could go on, I mean recollect with an impartial precision, I'll give it a shot,
the room bathed in light, ah, but are we back to that, back to YELLOW
once more, it can't be avoided it seems, ah, but if we had made love, or
'fucked' as she so charmingly put it, it would have killed me for sure, and
ON THE SPOT I'm talking about, but PERHAPS NOT, I'm just saying,
I mean this union of LOVE AND DEATH must be given some credence
or at any rate not summarily dismissed, I mean if one then the other or if
the other than the one with neither, please note, neither taking the UPPER
HAND, ah, but this is or was a moment to embrace, embellish, in other
words treasure, and let me just add the following, afterwards, and again this
notion of the passage of TIME a tricky one, but afterwards Anna fully,
completely, even surreally satisfied, and I the same of course, or DEAD, a
distinct possibility, and did I mention light, color, YELLOW to be specific,
the room, the hospital, the grounds, the city, the entire world flooded in
YELLOW, and our bodies as well of course, bathed in YELLOW, although
that was only mine perhaps, Anna' s a different hue, a mixture of pink,
white and gray if I'm not mistaken, but it all was or is remains to be seen,
imagined, which it was of course, but OH, WHAT A TIME WE HAD,
note the tense, but I'll end it here, there is no conceivable way to continue,
no, not after that.

    Neither here nor there.
Or neither now nor then.
Memory I'm talking about.
Or, 'Off they rode into the sunset.'
But who?
Precisely.
"Rachel, my love," I whispered.
Or Amanda, Lois or Eve.
Yes, Eve, the very first woman.

Yet how can one, how can I be sure?

The sights, the scents, the sounds after all these years.

Yes, I think I'm quite right in attempting to recall, although no doubt mistaken that I actually do.

The setbacks multiply.

Of course they do.

But was I or was I not a passionate man after all, and passionate where it counted the most, although, no, how can one ever be sure of something like that?

Time speeding up, slowing down, then speeding up once more.

In other words one proceeds.

Or 'lingers' might be more appropriate.

Yes.

The menace of strange mornings, afternoons, evenings, nights, ah, but how one would love to have things one way and not another, but the other, another persists with its cumbersome obstinacy, and then the YELLOW OF SPRING of course, it enters the heart, the mind, one's very veins, and, "Is this music I hear?" I screamed out the other night, waking from some dream no doubt, and the music itself distinct, precise and assaulting one's senses, Beethoven, yes, only Beethoven capable of such an assault on the senses, and just then I wanted to seize him by the throat and throttle him, yes, one of the all-time greats of music, and I wanted to rid myself not just of Beethoven but of ALL MUSIC then, the last thing I needed was to have MUSIC pursue me into my dreams, in my dreams and then out of them I was hanging on by a thread I felt and Beethoven, his MUSIC was cutting that thread, Beethoven smiled or scowled at me from a distance, 'Ah, but what a fragile, curious little creature you are,' he whispered, back in the dream his music turned into enormous red and black flowers that suffocated with their sickening smell, 'Let me tell you something,' the flowers whispered, 'the great unknown has you by the throat and you're not strong enough to resist, to fight back,' by then Beethoven was gone and his music no longer heard, only those whispering flowers remained, it was impossible to cut them down, to escape their noxious fumes, I soiled myself, of course, did you expect I wouldn't, "We'll have you cleaned up in no time," Anna bent over me, saying this she did a somersault over my bed, I would swear to it, 'You see how easy,' she even smiled, 'you simply have to make up your mind,' a fever burning inside me, my tumors chasing each other around my bed, 'Pay no attention,' Anna whispered, 'it's only spring fever,' she knew nothing about spring of course, she was simply guessing, theorizing, she had no idea spring could destroy as well as create, like MUSIC itself, in fact, 'But what about the music?' I yelled at her or thought I had, she took me by the hand then and led me about the room, as difficult to imagine as it is to relate, 'See, Viktor, see,' she pointed to the various objects around the room, 'you're safe and sound here, nothing will harm you because this is where you belong,' she initiated a game of tag then or catch-as-catch-can as I thought to myself, I would have preferred hide and-seek of course but there was no place to hide in that small room, in other words, please note, I had no CHOICE, absolutely none in the game we were to play, I chased after her the best I could, here we go, 'Come on, Viktor, you old fart, you miserable skeleton!' she even encouraged me, all in good fun of course, 'Ah, but this is the life,' I even thought to myself, if only my lungs and legs would hold out, if only I wouldn't stumble and shatter my bones into a million pieces, 'Come to mama, Viktor,' Anna smiled at me from a distance and spread herself like some human landscape, and here I should very much like to assert that I had an erection to end all erections but that would be going too far, even this hallucinatory event with certain built-in limitations, imagination bounded like everything else.

And burning up.

I was.

The fever scorching me like some human sacrifice.

Becoming more and more difficult.

To steady myself.

To keep things straight in my head.

"Don't fight it," I'm advised. "You're merely exhausting yourself."

By whom?

My wife, my last I can only assume, although by now I have neither the strength nor the wish to associate her with her name or her name with her.

"Ah, but you're nameless." I even smile at her.

It doesn't matter.

As far as I recall she was always a talker and not a listener, yes, hardly ever a listener, although right now I must admit to a certain degree of comfort or even pleasure, no, not pleasure, comfort let's just say in lying here and simply, merely listening, in other words in being both wordless and motionless, whereas she, here we go, is filled with both words and motion, trying for some sort of summation, yes, that's fairly obvious, or, yes, I think I've got it, trying to put things into some sort of PERSPECTIVE, 'Ah, but there are no more perspectives!' I mean to shout at her, 'All my perspectives shot to hell!' nothing comes out of course, I just hope you appreciate, my screams nothing but SCREAMS OF SILENCE, she is undeterred, she pushes on, one of her most or least endearing qualities as I recall, and, "Please, please," I hear between my screams of silence, "don't shut me out, not now, not at this final stage," in fact I almost pity her although that's a bit of an exaggeration, PITY at this stage of my dying not a particularly useful emotion, but let's just say I come numbingly, dangerously close, she pushes on, "Do you remember how you once told me that you wanted openness, nothing but openness in our relationship?" yes, someone may well have told her that although whether it was me or someone else no longer clear, "And that's all I'm asking for now, Viktor, that you be frank and open with me while there is still time, and I came here with the same intention, that I be totally frank and open with you, to hold nothing back, to tell you what's in my heart," ah, but this is turning out to be quite a confession, it most certainly is, and I just hope she expects no tit for tat, my so-called confession to accompany, to match hers, I'm not up to it, there is nothing but SILENCE left, "I don't know about you, Viktor, but throughout our life together I've put up with the most amazing insults, injuries and betrayals, Viktor, and all because I loved you, still do, because you were and still are my one and only," I blink, turn my head one way then another and blink at her, I mean what else, "and I know I should have had my head examined, even your friends, your friends forever telling me, 'But don't you know the kind of man you married? Haven't you realized it by now?' but I persisted, stayed the course, and now just tell me that in some way, your way you did the same, that my life with you, that our life together hasn't been a complete waste, that some something was genuine, real, that's all I need to know, Viktor, all I'm after."

Reasonable?

She certainly appears to be.

In other words this woman, whoever she is, is no one's fool but her own, as am I, in other words throughout my life no one's fool but my own, and I only wish I could say my heart goes out to her, it does in a way of course but in another, NO, yes, let's just be clear about this, my troubled, erratic, fibrillating heart stays right where it is for the time being, in other words in my troubled, erratic and fibrillating chest, I mean could anything be simpler, more obvious than this, but I have no way of getting this across to her, Samantha, yes, of course, and even if I did I'm not sure I would succeed.

Ah, but how we disappoint.

Ourselves, others, the entire world in fact.

And this is in time and with time but becoming especially obvious in retrospect, in other words with time running out, memory, ah, yes, memory the ultimate culprit in this, small wonder we run from it as if from the plague, death, here we go, yes, even into the very JAWS OF DEATH, yes, OBLIVION the last, the final, the only answer that remains, bear with me, but our backward glances, no matter how few and far between, disclose nothing but failures, disappointments and betrayals, except for a very few exceptions all of us masters at the art of failing, disappointing and betraying, yes, you might even say that all of us, with a few exceptions, born simply to fail, to disappoint and to betray, in other words whatever it takes to survive, the few exceptions, the Mozarts, the Beethovens, the Mahlers also born simply to fail, to disappoint and to betray, which they did of course in their day to day lives but, NO, not in their MUSIC, I just hope you see what I'm getting at, ah, but how tedious to have to explain, to take it upon oneself to try to explain, no matter, but those exceptional few SOMEHOW found or created a way to have their lives become and be about more than sheer survival, and this was in their MUSIC of course, it's their MUSIC I'm talking about, yes, but what about the rest of us, and, please, don't smile and nod or smile and shake your head, I mean if life is about nothing but SURVIVAL then it's truly about NOTHING AT ALL, this is as obvious to me as the gnarled fingers in front of my face, and in the end even SURVIVAL goes out the window, that's what I'm talking about, even that NOTHINGNESS goes out the window to be replaced by a GREATER, a MORE ENCOMPASSING NOTHINGNESS as far as we can tell, and if you think I'm on to nothing here you'd better think again, but who am I to tell you what and how to think, you're absolutely right, I'm just a drugged-up wreck on his way to TOTAL OBLIVION, no need to belabor the point, in fact no need to proceed in this fashion like scratching some festering wound only to have it fester and stink some more in the process.

Ah, here we go.

All the moans, groans and occasional screams from the other rooms, yes, at times they seem endless although now and again quite mesmerizing, yes, I'm sure a Mozart, a Beethoven or even a Mahler would know just what to do with them, I'm just saying, but, still, there is no escaping the reality that this is a building, an assembly line of death, that nothing blooms here but the flowers of dying and death, their very stink and colors in fact, their inimitable explosions, the cancerous growths, the bulbous tumors and open wounds with their grating ANTI-MUSIC although, please note, you don't hear me moaning, groaning and occasionally screaming in a similar fashion, in other words even if I'm incapable of creating TRUE MUSIC I'll be damned if I'll contribute to this melee this cacophony of ANTI-MUSIC, yes, even DEATH, even TOTAL OBLIVION preferable, in other words even if throughout my life I have been the cause of suffering in others, at least now I'm perfectly capable of suffering myself, and, mind you, in total or near total SILENCE, ah, if only that were really the case, but for argument's sake let's just say it is, as a matter of fact if I were ever to have a grave with a headstone, although I left quite specific, detailed instructions to the contrary, but if I ever were this is what I would like to see chiseled, engraved on it, AT LEAST IN THE END HE SUFFERED IN SILENCE, or change just a single word, AT LAST IN THE END HE SUFFERED IN SILENCE, yes, better I think, and I wouldn't even insist on the name, the dates, no, that inscription more than sufficient, but once again I'm getting off the topic, waylaying and or deserting myself, and we'll have none of that, no, it's way too late for that sort of nonsense.

Proceed.

The only thing left.

To continue as I've begun or never have, but here again a great deal of uncertainty, doubt as to TIME ITSELF, in other words by now my timing permanently off, shot to hell, past, present and future blending into a single IT WAS or IT IS, and I just hope I'm making this clear, although why it should be clear is beyond me, because CLARITY like TIME ITSELF is a gaping wound, an open question.

Restlessness.

Yes, that's good.

A certain restlessness.

And PERHAPS I've been restless all my life, I mean who's to say, but certainly, especially now, but, please note, no bitterness, no despair, no faith, no hope, I could go on, but NO ANGER, yes, that about covers it, as for the rest just this restlessness, which is open to interpretation, it most certainly is.

Here we go.

"Top of the morning," Anna greeted me the other day.

Or bottom or either of its sides, but, no, I was in no mood to complicate things just then, I mean geographically speaking, and glad, please note, actually GLAD to see her, and this without any accompaniment or even the possibility of an erection, yes, just simply glad, but by then NO SOUNDS, NO WORDS to convey this to her, a simple cough or the clearing of my throat was about all, and she went through her routine while I watched without participating, although I was dying, a curious wording, but I was just dying to say, to make some comment to her, yes, any number of things coming to my mind just then but a few examples should suffice, 'My, but how lovely you look this morning,' or, 'Have you done anything new to your hair?' or, 'Don't you look smart in that uniform?' you get the drift I think, but for various medical and or psychological reasons I was speechless and practically soundless by then, in other words all the sounds inside and none without, in other words trapped, fully trapped in myself by then much as I am in this sordid little room, but this is no complaint, absolutely not, just another of my partial or impartial observations, and at one point, at some other point, "What's the last thing you remember?" Anna asked, and then something even simpler, "How many fingers?" as she held up her hand, knowing full well I couldn't or wouldn't respond, in other words she was still playing our old game while I had already moved on to a new and different one, or perhaps NO GAME AT ALL, but, please, don't hold me to this, I'm simply using this exchange, which it really wasn't, as illustrative of my current and fast deteriorating state, yes, at this stage I have no wish to disguise, to hold back in any way, and, "What are we in the mood for today?" Anna finally asked, finished, ridiculous of course, all I could do was stare and nod, but let me end on a positive note, might as well, Anna's smile terrific, I don't know if I ever noticed it before or, if I have, took the trouble to mention it, I'm doing so now, and with that the world went blank, MY WORLD that is, and I groped uncertainly through the inner darkness.

Ah, but what a sordid little tale this is turning out to be.
Is it?
I leave it up to you.
But still some things left to be said or unsaid, done or undone, the world, MY WORLD mustn't be allowed to end in either a whimper or a bang but in SOME OTHER FASHION, help me out here, I hardly know myself, Anna still comes and goes as do all the others, both the living and the dead please note, both the LIVING and the DEAD, at and for the moment I am extending an open invitation to everyone who's had anything to do with my life, 'Come one, come all,' I'm thinking, 'and witness, have something to do with my dying, my death,' the response greater than you might imagine, the only question is what do with them, where to put them all as they crowd around my bed.

And, no, I no longer have anything to say to them, seriously, what is there left to say, and for their part they appear perfectly satisfied to simply mill about, to observe, yes, my dying, my death just another event in their lives, please note, THEIR LIVES, not MINE, recognition a problem of course, although not as difficult as you might imagine, in other words not entirely insurmountable, and names, ah, here we go, even some of their names come to me although I really have no way to check on the validity, the accuracy of this, and, 'Make yourself comfortable,' I even say to them, which under the circumstances is nothing short of remarkable, I think you'll agree, a good time had by all I'm even tempted to think, although no, that's going a bit too far, a time then, yes, simply SOME KIND OF TIME had by all.

And spring explodes.

Yes.

Nothing like spring to cut to the chase, to the very heart of the matter, in other words spring does an about-face, turns on its own axis to face LIFE not DEATH, I only wish I could do the same, spring with everything to gain and nothing to lose, I think you understand, the sun strong and the moon weak, or perhaps it's the other way around, the clouds drifting singly or in pairs, seen from a distance it's impossible to tell at times, but you see, I just hope you see how I'm still looking for ways to observe and accurately describe although that's getting more and more difficult, no question, but let me just say this, I continue, carry on, in other words in some fashion or other I still PROCEED, ah, but how exhilarating just to pretend that I am, beating time at its own game I'm tempted to say, but, no, never happen, COOPERATING WITH TIME TO THE VERY END let's just say, and now and again, ah, here we go, MUSIC, which I both do and don't hear, I mean it's hard to tell, but not my own, please note, NOT MY OWN, Mozart's, Beethoven's, Mahler's, I mean here they are keeping me company to the bitter end, sonatas, concertos and even a few symphonies, although no entire works, absolutely not, a few passages or even just chords is all, but the thing, the main thing is I recognize them, almost, please, ALMOST as though I had COMPOSED THEM MYSELF, but let's not get carried away, but the music, THEIR MUSIC penetrates ever deeper into whatever remains of my consciousness, I even hum along although that's questionable, and I'm thinking, 'Perhaps this is the end' although not in so many words, no, musically speaking let's just say, and what happens next is anybody' s guess, in other words up for grabs, in other words I just don't know what happens next.

Who was it who?

Or when was it when?

But we said goodbye at the station, but let's change the tense, from the past to the past participle or even the ever present, legitimate I think, let's start again, we were or are saying goodbye at the station, and feel free to imagine an embrace such as often occurs in situations like this, but just who is leaving and who staying behind is not at all clear, yes, even the identities questionable, not mine of course, for the purposes of recollection we can safely assume that I AM I, we'll go on, from this little scene, this image it's fairly clear we are loath to let each other go, to abandon each other to our separate fates, although not entirely, in other words we both do and don't, ah, but there is nothing like a good parting to clear things up or to complicate them, in other words in leaving each other what else but find each other and in finding what else but leave each other behind, and if you expect this to get any simpler it won't, it NEVER WILL, I'll add something else to this recollection, if that's what it is, there are no words, is that right, nothing spoken, ah, but are we finally done with words, one can only hope, we stand in a white cloud, steam in other words, but to be more precise we appear, disappear then reappear in that white cloud, in that steam, and how's this for setting a scene, an image, I just hope you realize that to the very end I'M DOING MY BEST, yes, I'm asking for no more than a bit of recognition, and there or here we're done I'd like to think, although not just yet, no sense jumping the gun, SOMETHING still remains, I leave it to you, but something still remains.

Spring.
Let's just stay with this.
Focus on this.
In other words the evidence of life all around.
Do I still have your attention?
Birds for example.
Just now or then but now will do, pigeons for example, lined up, neatly, on my windowsill, and from this, from my vantage point they resemble notes, musical notations, and I can not only see, read but hear them as well, please, don't interrupt, MUSIC TO DIE BY I'm tempted to say, in other words if not to live at least to die by, Anna enters my room, ah, here we go, she appears a little off balance but perhaps it's the other way around, yes, I'm sure it is, ah, but it's too late, everything too late by now, she stretches out a hand of greeting or warning, I only wish I knew, says something I can't

make out, no matter, changes, ah, but what sort, but all kinds of changes taking place, but once again I must insist on leaving this to you, and Anna wearing some kind of flowered or flowery dress, wrong, absolutely, but it no longer matters, and, please note, memory, vision, hearing, smelling, tasting and so on all shot to hell although SOMETHING of the imagination still remains, and with spring in the air and Anna in her flowery dress you may well ask if I, we are finally reaching the end, here, I'll put it another way, are we finally up against the miracle of life or of death or of some mind-bending combination of the two, please, don't frown or shake your head, you must see how I'm still trying to do MY BEST, which isn't good enough, no, it never was, but now it simply MAKES NO DIFFERENCE, as a matter of fact I breathe a bit easier now than before, say two or three minutes ago, ah, but how DECEPTIVE it all is, even in the end, and then there's shit and piss and vomit which I can no longer see or smell or taste, but, ah, yes, still imagine, let's just hope it'll get somewhat better than this, I press against the darkness, enchanting to say the least, mind you, there's no reason for you to take my word for any of this, not before and certainly not now, ah, but the music, a suite, and I'm reaching, I know, but what else but reach for SOMETHING in the end, enveloped in sound, you see how simple, how easy in the end, and even if the significance and or insignificance escapes me, THERE IS NO MORE REASON TO CHASE AFTER IT, and all my loves, my lost loves just a single love then, they dance to the gurgling in my throat, and, 'Come, follow,' they all smile, and I do, not that I have a choice, but OF COURSE I FOLLOW IN THE END.